BURNING MOON

"...is an uncommonly good thriller, full of excitement all the way. I was impressed by the way the authors handled the outdoor scene, and the final surprise delighted me."—JOHN GODEY, author of THE TAKING OF PELHAM ONE, TWO, THREE

BURNING MOON

"The characters make BURNING MOON really stick....What makes it so enjoyable is not just the twists, not just the chases, the dialogue of the characters is the seasoning."—THE FRESNO BEE

BURNING MOON

"Thrill-packed....It wouldn't be fair to even hint at the ending, which turns out to be quite surprising for all hands."—OREGON JOURNAL

BURNING MOON

"...A fine evening's escape, a literal cliff-hanger with a startling finish...remarkable suspense."
—SAN FRANCISCO BAY GUARDIAN

BURNING MOON

"A darn good action story and a really unexpected ending."—IDAHO STATE JOURNAL

BURNING MOON

ARON SPILKEN and ED O'LEARY

PLAYBOY PRESS
PAPERBACKS

Acknowledgments

Jonelle Brown
Terry Kime
Margaret Kilkauley
Mary Heslin
Linda Trees
Lillibil Olsen
Florence McNulty
Anna Altshuler

From the back you couldn't tell her height because she was so hunched. Ruth sat in the center bay window of her living room, silhouetted and still, at her small desk. Her left arm propped her cheek-bone on a shelf of knuckles. She was contained and totally concentrated. The tightness of the position released some of the tension in her body. She would write several lines, stop to consider how far she had come and how far she had to go, and then write again, smoothly and firmly:

Dear Posey,

I am very sad as I write and think of you. Because if you are reading this then it means my plans have not gone as I hoped and this is our good-bye. That stops me. Death itself is enormous enough, but leaving you seems somehow even larger to me. Ah, well, this is only a letter. It won't hold all I feel and all I have to tell you. So I will just have to do the best I can and trust you to understand in your own way.

The first thing I must tell you is that I am not doing this for you. I am doing it for myself. If I were only thinking of you I would just keep going to my job at the Basket every day. I would stay in San Francisco and take care of you as long as you needed it. I would do very little of anything else for the next fifteen years or so. When I decided to let you grow in me and become a person in the world I thought I would do that. I thought that watching you grow and become strong and free from the doubts and fears I have lived with— I thought that would be enough for me. It is not. I don't love you any less than I did. I love you much, much more than when I made that decision. But I made that decision without knowing what I know now. One person cannot live just for another, no matter how much they love them. I have been at The Yellow Basket for two years now. I work without any special thought or feeling for fifty weeks of every year. Then I have two weeks of my life to do what I want. Somehow I have managed to learn nothing else. I can look forward only to small raises and a few more days added to my vacation time. And I have to wait years for even that.

I am not trying to excuse myself. What I am going to do is wrong. I have always believed it was wrong to take things that belong to another person or to hurt someone. I still believe that, and I expect I will have to pay in some way for going against my conscience, even if I am successful. But I have reached a point where the hopelessness I feel in my life for myself is even more painful. So I have made my choice, I feel responsible for it, and

like every other part of my life, I will go ahead
in the very best way I know how.

Have I explained anything? Do you understand? I am not afraid of your anger. I am
even pleased imagining that you disapprove.
No, what I want to do is spare you the burden, the special kind of self-hate which comes
from hating a parent. I want you to know that
I am not so different from anyone else, that I
do good and bad while mostly wanting to do
good, like other people you know. And while
you may think anything you want about what
I do, you have no reason to be ashamed of me
as a parent or as a person. I do love you.

Mom

When she was done she read it through twice,
then she folded it and sealed it in an envelope.
The gesture was meant to bring that moment to
a close. But her feelings didn't fade so rapidly. She
sat there, time passing, looking around the room,
until she saw she still had the envelope in her
hand and had to decide where to leave it.

Friday 7:30 P.M.

"Okay. Everything's in the van but this. I'll take the list and you pack. I'll call off each item, you put it in, and I'll check it off."

"Right," Alice agreed.

"The last thing we need is to get all the way up there and find out that we've forgotten something."

"Right," Alice said again, patiently.

She sat by the pile on the living room floor and looked up expectantly, her dark eyes serious behind their lenses. The cut of her straight dark hair lent a slight resemblance to Billie Jean King, whom she admired. She was a medium-looking young woman: medium height, medium weight, medium coloring, or perhaps slightly olive, now well tanned on her face and hands. Her hands were strong-looking and quite rough for a city woman; used, not ornamental. She took off her glasses and rubbed her tired eyes. Exposed like that they were large, doelike, and soft. More like her voice. But they were balanced by a strong chin.

"One dress, one skirt and top, one gown," Ruth read. Her voice was sharp, thin like her body. She was between five-seven and five-eight, but she was the type of person who always seems much taller than she actually is. She was light-skinned, pale to rose, with a dandelion fluff of tight curls on top of a long stem. And she was about eight years older than Alice.

"Check." Alice folded the garments into the suitcase, a cheap Goodwill item picked up for the trip only the day before.

"Three pair of snazzy, jazzy, hot-momma heels," Ruth listed without real humor.

"Check."

"Four pair of panty hose."

"Yep."

"Black wig, blond wig, auburn wig."

Alice nodded as she looked under the lid of each hatbox. She pulled the guns from the pile and placed them expectantly in front of her.

"Let's do them last," Ruth said, looking at the brown canvas-wrapped parcels. "How about the 'Natural You Complete Traveling Cosmetic Bag'?" she asked.

"Everything for the modern woman on the go," Alice agreed, tucking the flowered plastic sack into a corner of the suitcase.

"Three pairs of falsies." She scowled involuntarily.

"Shawls. Feather boa."

"Three sets of earrings, one imitation gold chain and pearl choker, one simulated silver and turquoise squash blossom, one slave ankle bracelet, and one assorted handful of cute, trendy rings. That ought to get them. And now"—Ruth gestured toward the floor—"two AR-7 Explorer Survival Rifles, and ammunition for same. For women on the rise."

"And that ought to really get them," she added

seriously while Alice packed the parcels carefully and without a word.

The AR-7 Explorer Survival Rifle is a civilian version of a weapon the air force originally designed to be dropped with pilots into the wilderness. The man in the gun shop hadn't seemed to think it was much of a gun. Not a gunman's gun, his looks said. "It will do what it's supposed to do," he told them, his tone disparaging. "As a weapon it is superior to throwing rocks." When they decided to buy two anyway, he accepted the order with a shrug and a look that said simply, "Women. You can't tell them anything."

But they had decided. The guns were light, only two and three-quarter pounds each, not a bad weight for carrying a distance. And most important of all, they broke down, a feature which made them unique in over-the-counter arms. Barrel, action, and clip fit snugly into the stock, a mere sixteen and one-half inches long—short enough to be stowed easily in their oversized summer bags.

It was enough to make you stop and think. They did, and they were still doing it when a child's heavy shoes came pounding down the hallway. "Is it time yet? Are we going?" she called from the door.

Ruth ran thin fingers tensely through her curly blond hair. "Are you ready to go, Posey? We're almost done."

"Can I bring my books?" the three-year-old asked earnestly.

"You can bring three of them. Pick the three you like the best and let's go. She'd take every damn book in the house if I didn't tell her that," Ruth explained, still distracted by her thoughts. "Well, I

guess that's it," she sighed after a moment. Alice
sighed too, not really aware she was mimicking
her friend. She shut the suitcase carefully and
stood up.

Ruth looked around her living room in conflict,
part of her wanting to give in to a sudden sadness,
wanting to say good-bye to everything, and another
side of her, rational and practical, impatient with
these feelings and wanting to get on with it. They
were in a cheerful Victorian flat in the Noe Valley
district of San Francisco, airy and light, windows
at the front. There were bright little paintings and
hangings scattered about and many plants. Would
the plants be all right? What difference would that
make if she were not all right, if she never made
it back to see them again? It would make a difference, she decided. Propped on the mantel was the
sealed envelope addressed to her daughter. "Let's
go!" she called forcefully toward the bedrooms at
the back.

"I just want to bring these crayons too," Posey
announced as she struggled into the room with her
load of books, dolls, and toys.

Alice picked up the suitcase and the wig boxes
and went quietly out to the beige VW van parked
downstairs in front of the house. Ruth knelt down
and sorted through Posey's armload, paring it to a
size which could be transported to the baby-sitter's
and leaving the peelings in a pile on the floor.
Then, holding hands and sharing the load, they
carefully climbed down the stairs to the slightly
battered van and got in. Ruth cranked the engine
over, keeping its hesitant pulse going by pumping
the gas pedal energetically. She headed down
Vicksburg, turned into the traffic on Twenty-fourth

Street, and then went uphill toward Diamond Heights and the baby-sitter's.

Indian summer, the only warm San Francisco season, had not come yet. Above them she could see the blinking red lights of the new Sutro TV tower. It was particularly huge and ugly. While they were building it, she had taken revenge with daydreams of bombing it off the horizon.

"Bud's," her daughter pointed out the landmark knowingly, pressing a fingertip against the glass. Attuned to the mood of the day, she made no attempt to ask for a cone. The usual Friday-night crowd was waiting, patiently lined up around the corner and up the block, ice-cream freaks who would have laughed in your face if you told them this was no weather for ice cream. They rode up the hill, past the Meat Market, their favorite coffeehouse, where it all began.

They were shivering a bit, in a way they were used to, as they bundled into Mrs. Van Nostrand's. "Now, when can I expect to hear from you, Ruth?" Mrs. Van Nostrand asked as they worked together at getting Posey settled in.

"I'll try to call in about five days. But please don't worry if you don't hear from us right away. We'll be all right. The Canadian woods aren't like the city. Sometimes things happen and you have to slow down or go a different way than you'd planned, or the weather can do things. . . . Oh, that reminds me," and she raised both hands in pantomimed eagerness, the picture of someone with an important message they want to get just right. "Posey's birthday is on the twenty-first. She'll be three years old. Finally!" She gave an exasperated laugh, still playing mother for Mrs. Van Nostrand.

"I'm going to be sure to be back for that. I wouldn't miss it for anything. But just in case we had car trouble, or anything like that, and were delayed, I wanted to be sure she would have something. So I wrote her a little letter and left it on the mantel. Now that I've told you, you can forget about it. It's not to be opened before her birthday, so I'm sure you won't need it. Just being careful. Do you understand?" she asked.

"Of course I do," Mrs. Van Nostrand reassured her. "I'm not completely ignorant." She opened her hands, presenting her plump little body in its cotton print dress as evidence. "Although when I was growing up women didn't go off on their own to do these things. But then we missed out on a lot of experiences, I suppose."

"We just like to get out in the woods," Alice explained. "It keeps us healthy, and in a better frame of mind."

"Well, you two should be in an excellent frame of mind with all the hiking you've been doing lately. So I won't worry about you, and don't you worry about us, either. Enjoy your vacation. Take your time and have a good rest. Or a good hike. Or whatever you're supposed to have in the woods," she finished good-naturedly.

"My mommy has a gun," Posey announced.

There was a brief flash of silence which froze them for the instant.

"Gum, dear, gum," Ruth corrected her, and rummaged in her purse for a piece of gum.

"I have some chewing gum," Mrs. Van Nostrand offered, "but I didn't think you let her have that."

"Only once in a while. For a treat," Ruth explained. "Good-bye, dear." Ruth bent down and

hugged her daughter. "Good-bye, Mrs. Van Nostrand," she said, still looking at Posey. "See you
in about two weeks. And I'll call as soon as I can."
The four of them kept up a steady volley of good-
byes all the way down to the van. And even after
she had started the motor, Ruth rolled down her
window to wave at the two forms in the doorway,
the light behind them so she couldn't see their
faces any longer, the little one already in bunny
pajamas. "Good-bye, dear," she called for the last
time, suddenly feeling horribly mournful. She
swung the machine quickly downhill to escape the
feeling and headed for the Army Street entrance
to the freeway.

How do we ever get to where we are? Ruth wondered. If someone had told me, five, six years ago,
"Look, you've got to be in this particular situation
in this amount of time," I would have been sure it
was impossible. But it *is* me, right here.

Six years ago she had still been married. To
"what's-his-name," as she always called him with
her friends. A nice enough person, but after six
long years it was still all she could say about him.
And what a drama it had seemed to be, way back
then.

She had married young, back in Omaha, without
a thought. She had actually cleaned the house and
watched the soaps, so she knew for a fact that
that was a real way of life, something some people
really did. What's-his-name had been totally confused when she asked for a separation. He was
working his ass off, she had everything, what else
did she want, and didn't she consider the possibility that she might be just a little neurotic? Yes,
she had considered it. She actually believed in such

things back in those days. She was sure that was the reason she so often felt she was suffocating. Neurosis, of course. . . .

"But something is still wrong," she told him. "I can feel it even if I don't know what it is. I just want some time to think. That doesn't seem so unreasonable."

"Forget the separation," he decided abruptly. "If we're going to do this, let's do it right. If I'm not enough for you, get a divorce so you can do what you really want." He was convinced her vagueness was a cover-up. She wanted more action, the freedom to run around. It was the only thing that made sense. He went through her pockets for love notes, motel receipts, anything which would make it understandable to him. But that wasn't to be, and they parted with him unsoothed, still angry and hurt, and Ruth now feeling bored with him in a way she knew would be permanent.

She had tried a junior college, taken some art classes, met some new people. She had had an affair with a married man, thinking it would be an interesting thing to try, like a new food. There was so much fuss about it in the magazines she read. As if it were important in some way. It wasn't, although it did go on for almost a year.

Then she had a sudden, clear, and complete realization: relationships didn't work. Even with the best will in the world—and both men had been good people—they couldn't give you what you really needed. Anything she wanted she now knew she would have to get for herself. That was when she had gotten pregnant.

She didn't tell him. Or anyone else. She came instead to San Francisco. It was her choice, her child, and she didn't want that confused by any sentiment or social pressure.

She still had her mother in Omaha. She and her mother exchanged cards on the holidays and a few letters during the year. Her mother didn't know about Posey. If she did she would have been there in an instant. But she never seemed to think of coming only to see Ruth. Well, that was just fine for the time being. Maybe they would all get together later on. And maybe not.

"We're on our way," Alice said when they finally crammed into the crowd on the freeway. The beginning of the weekend traffic around them was moving at an erratic "city" pulse, darting in and out to squeeze any advantage of inches or seconds. But Ruth had already settled down to her highway pace, a steady sixty miles per hour which shaded the limit a fraction but was still within the safe shadow of it. She sat in the middle of her lane and headed straight for the Bay Bridge with its hypnotic length and regularity.

"Seventeen hours from now we should be leaving Salt Lake City," Alice announced, stacking the necessary maps in the proper order and folding the first one open to the West Coast. A wide path of orange magic marker wound up Highway 80 through Sacramento, on through Donner Pass in the Sierra Nevada, and then down toward Reno and off the map. "And in twenty-two hours: Norman and the Cowboy Bar in Jackson, Wyoming. I wonder how he'll like it." She had been trying to sound crisp and efficient, her own way of dealing with her feelings about finally starting off. But when she laughed, her voice returned naturally to its usual softness and warmth.

"And I wonder how I'll like it," Ruth said.

"The Cowboy Bar? Oh, you'll like it, you'll like it," Alice assured her.

"Do you want to get some sleep?"

"Not yet. I'm too wide awake. It's only eight-thirty."

At the mention of time Ruth instinctively leaned forward and scanned the sky. Alice did the same and the two women peered upward seriously for several minutes without a word. Their faces seemed a bit strained and not especially pleased. There was not a single sign of the moon through the coastal overcast.

Friday 8:00 P.M.

Jackson Lake Lodge was large and luxurious and still very much linked to the Rockefeller family. Upstairs was a huge guest lounge, enormous fireplaces, and an expansive view of the mountains. It was the waiting area for the lecture halls and the dining rooms. A massive staircase led directly down to the large lobby.

Norman was busy. Up and down, back and forth, he paced. Through the high-columned lobby of Jackson Lake Lodge, along the main stairs at the back, even nosing behind the stairs, through the double doors and into the service tunnel with its butcher shop and laundry and bakery, poking into every cranny to familiarize himself with what was there and who was where. All the time with one hand in his pocket, like some habitual masturbator, clutching his secret stopwatch, clicking off times, checking distances, clocking the security guard.

"Please, could I help you?"

"Huh?" Deeply concentrating, he had been startled by the voice at his shoulder.

"I noticed you wandering around and I wondered if you were looking for something."

It was the information hostess, guardian spirit

20

of the lobby. She was also the very last person he wanted to meet now. "I was, uh, I uh . . . ," he fumbled, completely off-balance for the moment as he thought of the possible complications. Instinctively he also lowered his voice and hung his head to avoid her direct scrutiny as much as possible.

"It's right back there, next to the stairs, along the wall," she told him professionally.

"Uh, thank you," he replied and moved directly off.

"Just past the ladies' room, on the same side," she called after him before turning to a confused-looking couple in the center of the lobby.

Norman's watch told him it was almost lecture time but he still had one more thing to check before then, something he had been saving for just this moment. Instead of walking past the ladies' room, as he had been directed, he turned left. Opposite it, leading under the stairs, was a similar door. He pushed through, already starting to fumble with his fly, head down, zipper descending, his momentum carrying him well into the office before his face registered where he was, or more to the point, wasn't. It wasn't the men's room. There was office furniture all around and a mild little man in a smaller office branching off the main one looked up to see his obvious embarrassment. Norman took a quick look around. "It's across the hall," the man answered without waiting to be asked. "On the same side as the ladies' room, but further down." Norman gruffly thanked him as he backed right out.

Then, satisfied, he hurried up the stairs to the lecture hall. The front rows were almost full, but there was room in the rear. Quite a few doctors were already back there, leaving an empty chair or two between them on which they threw their suit jackets. People who liked to sprawl liked to take off their jackets whenever they could. Everything was as it should be.

Norman chose his seat carefully, climbing over the necessary knees with the necessary apologies until he was properly situated between two discarded coats. He pulled out his pad and fussed a minute, busy searching for his pen while the physicians around him looked him over. He met no one's eye. He didn't look familiar to them but he made himself serious and that was enough. Then he rested his head in one hand, covering his eyes with his fingers, slowly massaging his forehead as if he were tired or had a headache. Behind his hand he kept his eyes closed.

He did not look up when he heard two more sets of steps enter, the door shutting behind them. Someone walked to the back of the room, to the raised projection booth. The other one walked to the front, to the podium. "Good evening." He heard a firm, pleasant woman's voice from the front. "On behalf of Jackson Lake Lodge I'd like to welcome you to this meeting of the Western States Medical Association. I'm Diane Greene, ranger-naturalist, and I'll be conducting your seminars on mountain medicine. We'll have part one tonight. We'll take a break tomorrow, when you'll be having your cocktail party, I believe. And we'll meet here again on Sunday evening for part two. Why don't we start off by taking a look at our subject. . . ."

Norman heard a sharp click-clack, a mechanical "cricket" to signal the projectionist. He felt the light dim against his eyelids and heard the slide projector answer with a quick scraping sound of its own. The scene was from the broad back terrace of the lodge. The wide-angle view showed Willow Flats, green and moist, and the Teton wall rising in all its Ektachromatic brilliance in the background. The gray of the granite and white of the snow were set off by a dark blue polarized sky and a few bright shreds of clouds. There were probably some moose feeding on the willows in the foreground, but Norman was still careful not to look.

Again Diane Greene pressed the metal clicker in her hand and again the answering noise came from the background. To Norman it was as if giant insects were seeking each other in the summer night for some crashing copulation.

The mountains leaped abruptly forward, in close-up view now, filling the screen with their stone shoulders and forcing the lowland meadow from the bottom of the frame. It was Mount Moran, the telescopic close-up showing the huge solid rock, almost seamless from base to crest, and the sheer walls of the ascent.

"You can see they're very beautiful," Diane said into the darkness. It was torture for Norman. He was always eager to look when someone wanted to show him something.

"But in addition to being beautiful they're very accessible as well. And when you have to look at them in terms of the park's rescue-and-treatment responsibilities, they look like a colossal pain in the butt. It's the combination of attractiveness and accessibility that is the problem," she explained, clicking again. "Because they are so easy to get to, almost anyone can go into these mountains. And many of those who go are uninformed and unprepared. Now that's disastrous. This season there were three deaths. We had to perform forty-three rescue operations. And that was in the short period of only eighty days."

The camera zoomed in still closer to a trail running along a sheltered ledge high in the mountains. Only in this picture there was a person. What looked at first like a person. A man was lying on the ground, huddled, knees drawn up, his head on one arm. He wore expensive hiking clothes, new-looking and stylishly colorful. But his face was ashen, blue gray, the same cyanotic tinge which darkened his fingers and lips. In delicate contrast a pale pink fluid oozed from his nose and mouth, with a light froth of bubbles still stuck to his lips. He was recently dead and the doctors saw that he didn't look very different from a man who had drowned, or suffered pulmonary edema with cardiac failure. A common enough death.

"I'm sure you recognize the signs of high-altitude pulmonary edema," Diane said quietly, and paused to let them look a moment at the man whose lungs had failed him. "It's either weather or, as in this picture, altitude which causes the problems. Most of our weather comes over the top of the mountains and drops down on us, suddenly. Sometimes the temperature can fall twenty or more degrees in less than an hour. Clear skies can turn to rain and lightning, and perfect visibility can become snow or a dense, soaking fog impossible to hike in. And then with predictable regularity, somewhere in the mountains there is a solitary hiker or couple, or a small group, who are surprised to find they are in serious trouble, or sometimes actually dying."

She stopped to let that sink in, to penetrate her own feelings as well as theirs. It was too easy to become practiced and automatic at lecturing, and to lose the real meaning of what was happening.

"I've seen that look of surprise too many times. And I think that's the true lesson for us. That look says that danger came unsuspected to people who felt confident and safe, to people who were hiking in beautiful mountains, breathing clean, fresh air, to people who couldn't have imagined a more healthy and happy experience.

"So I won't be talking about climbing accidents, although we have more than we would like. Because a fall from a rock isn't so different from a fall from a scaffold or a construction site. Except perhaps in terms of rescue. And the climbers, bless 'em, go out there knowing there is danger on the rock. But the effects of altitude and mountain weather can be something totally different, something less known and more sinister, which claim many who never looked for thrills or danger. So this weekend I'll be reviewing with you the two most dangerous mountain sicknesses: tonight, high-altitude pulmonary edema, and on Sunday, hypothermia. We'll have some case histories for illustration."

Norman had been trying to follow her words but it was too big a drain on his attention. His business had begun in earnest when the lights went out. Because his eyes were covered up till that moment, he was already dark-adapted. In fact he was probably the only one in the room who could see in the sudden blackness. And he was careful not to look at the screen, the mountain slides which held everyone else's attention, so he wouldn't be blinded again by the glare. He slipped his left hand out and into the coat on that side. Better work the left first, he decided. He was right-handed. If there were any left-handed clumsiness it would be shielded by the first darkness and the initial interest in the slides. It went quickly. He found the plastic square which held the doctor's convention name tag, unclipped the safety pin which held it to the breast pocket, palmed it, and withdrew. It dropped out of sight into his shirt pocket.

From such little things identities were made. The standard practice was to cross out the doctor's first name and write in the woman's name by hand. And presto: doctor's wife! The tags were impossible to read and yet when the women walked about in the lobby they could give great security and guarantee the utmost courtesy and cooperation from the staff. Norman decided to cross out the names himself before he turned them over to the women. He didn't trust them to pick good names. He would write in "Vera" and "Pauline," he decided, pleased with his choices. Now he needed the other tag.

"Let's take a look at some actual cases," Diane was saying from the front. She turned a page in her notes. "Arnold Brown," she announced to the group, as if they must remember the case, a classic. "A thirty-two-year-old Seattle businessman, an experienced weekend hiker and cross-country skier, brought his family to the Tetons for a week's vacation. His wife and two small children camped on the valley floor while he went into the mountains with some friends for several days' hiking." She paused, took a breath, wondering was it really necessary to go into this? Surely they knew how it would all turn out.

"Within the first few hours he was already feeling headache, dizziness, fatigue, shortness of breath, loss of appetite, and slight nausea. He rightly recognized the symptoms as typical mountain sickness. Brown had had similar difficulties in the past, and they had subsided as he became acclimatized, as his body adjusted to the decreased oxygen at higher altitudes.

"He was mistaken, though, when he told his friends he would be fine because he was in excellent physical condition. Contrary to popular belief, physical fitness gives no protection against mountain sickness and doesn't help in acclimatization. Neither does the fact that he had previously been at that altitude without any difficulty. Nor is youth any insurance, in this case. The age range from the preteens to the thirties seems to be struck most of all. But apparently neither he, nor any of his friends, all experienced hikers, were aware of this.

"They continued climbing, carrying heavy packs and spending their time hiking and camping between eight thousand and eleven thousand feet, a significant but hardly extreme height. On the afternoon of the second day breathing felt more difficult and weakness became a real problem for him. His party made camp by a sheltered spot on a ridge at about eleven thousand feet. They were concerned about him and would have already started the return hike to the valley floor if they hadn't thought he needed more rest.

"Late that day he developed a dry cough and continued to grow weaker. By evening they heard gurgling sounds in his chest and then he began to cough up bloody sputum. He wasn't comfortable lying down but was soon too weak to sit up. That made his breathing even more difficult. His friends did all they could to keep him warm, gave him hot fluids, and let him rest, in the mistaken impression that he had pneumonia. During the night he lost consciousness."

Damn! thought Norman. The other one had been easy. The jacket had just been lying there neatly folded with the name tag on top. A few tight seconds wondering if his arm was really as invisible to the man on his left as it seemed to be . . . and then it was over. But this jacket on his right was another matter entirely. He cursed himself now for not examining it more closely before the lights went out. It was bunched and twisted in some way he couldn't figure out. Just when he thought he had found a familiar seam or pocket, knew where he was and where he was headed, he came upon more folds which shouldn't be there, and no breast pocket.

It seemed as if he had been traveling on his fingertips through this maze of cloth for hours. Heavy material. Harris Tweed, he guessed, from the surface coarseness. For the evening cool which never left the mountains. He was getting impatient, but he kept himself from hurrying. It wouldn't do to suddenly shift some keys or loose change. All he needed was to be arrested as a sneak thief. His fingers bunched around handfuls of fabric, squeezing gently through the layers which hid their secrets so successfully from him, seeking the sharp outlines of that plastic square which held the doctor's convention ID card.

"As soon as there was enough light someone

went down the mountain to get help. I might add that this rescuer fell while hurrying and broke his arm during the descent; in the mountains injury or danger to one person often results in serious trouble for others. An emergency rescue party was organized in a rush down below. In their eagerness to help, no one realized the need to bring at least one experienced person with the group. A helicopter was flown to the ridge. No one thought to bring oxygen, or even realized it was necessary. Friends and helpers swarmed over the unconscious Arnold Brown doing their misguided best to save him. During the evacuation, possibly from the greater altitude of the helicopter flight, or possibly just through the normal progress of the disease, Mr. Brown suffocated."

She could see their faces dimly in the reflected light from the screen. Faces and necks, pale lightbulb shapes, glowing faintly like ideas as if to show her each was a distinct little bubble of consciousness. They seemed interested, as far as she could tell. At least they were quiet, not talking or fidgeting, facing toward her and the pictures of the mountains alongside of her. And they might remember the technical information she was giving. But not like they would remember if they had actually been with her as she waited with Brown's wife as the rescue helicopter brought him back down.

"As you know, the causes of high-altitude pulmonary edema are still unexplained. We do know that fluid is deposited in the lung and it blocks the transfer of oxygen from the air. Victims smother, or drown, in their own juices. It usually strikes unacclimatized individuals who climb rapidly and engage in heavy physical effort soon after arriving at high altitudes. If he had been less convinced he was fit, and had been less inclined to drive himself, the entire episode might had been avoided. And if his symptoms had only been recognized, and if instead of bedding him down his friends had helped him descend a mere two or three thousand feet, it probably would have saved his life." She was ready now for the blackboard. She signaled for the lights.

Norman jumped! His right hand popped out of the jacket and the man sitting next to it turned and examined him. "Dropped my name tag," Norman said foolishly. He picked it up from the floor where it had flown, showed the man the back of it quickly, then popped it into his shirt pocket with the other. If the man were suspicious and asked to see it he could switch and show him the other man's. If he remembered which was which. The man said nothing.

What a lousy slide show, Norman complained to himself, trying to rest, to settle down now that his work was over and he was free to relax for a while. Lousy slide show. A few mountains and then pop, on with the lights. There were no complaints from the rest of the audience. If you tried a stunt like that with a room full of kids you'd have screaming, stamping, and popcorn throwing. These people looked too stuffy for that, he decided.

The talking went on, pouring back in a steady stream from the front of the room, but he couldn't be bothered. He had never been very good at sitting still and being talked at. Nothing personal against the speaker. She was a ranger in her thirties. She had the kind of full, firm voice which comes from someone who is relaxed and at ease with herself. Dark hair almost straight to her shoulders, not stylish but not neglected either. Strong body, a bit more than average height, and a sturdy bone structure. She moved on the podium giving an impression of balance, solidness, dependability. Typical of the kinds of women and men he saw in the mountains, people who liked the outdoors and the physical work and the self-reliance the area demanded of those who stayed. The place was so suited to deer and elk and moose that those who lived there came to resemble them. She would have seemed more at home outside. She didn't appear that thrilled about doing the lecture.

Well, he hated to do this, but he had to go. He stood up and began sliding out of his row. Almost immediately he started a sequence of "excuse me" 's which seemed to echo until he was out the door, down the stairs, and headed for the parking lot.

The fresh air awakened Norman. He rolled the window down, even though it was cold, and headed the station wagon north. The gas station closed at nine. By the time he got there it should be dark, shut for the night, and unattended. This was a pretty road, partly remembered and partly seen. There was light coming from somewhere. No visible moon, but it might be behind him. The sky was brighter than the trees and the mountains which it outlined. He passed dense stands of lodge-pole pine, thin and straight, alternating with open meadows.

After five miles he came to a turnoff. Coulter Bay was on the two-lane road to the left. He sat in the dark and empty intersection orienting himself for the moment. Twenty miles straight ahead was the south gate of Yellowstone. Only twelve miles in that direction was Flagg Ranch, where raft trips left for the chute through Flagg Canyon. A hairy ride in the spring, but dull to nonexistent this late in the year. On his left, before the crotch of the road fork, was the gas station.

It looked empty. Norman needed the gas station. He couldn't park along the roadside or rangers would be sure to investigate. The high crime of national-park life was someone sleeping in a vehicle not in a regulation campground. But parked in the gas station there would be no trouble.

He eased the big car into the adjoining lot. He turned the motor off and sat a minute. No sign of life. Fine. He took a small wrench and screwdriver from the glove compartment and cautiously let himself out.

Twenty yards into the dark he came upon a sign which warned: PRIVATE ROAD—National Park Service Employees Only. His antennae were out now, probing for any presence, any sound or movement on the road ahead or in the woods around him. After a quarter-mile the road opened into a large paved lot.

A small white building in the near corner had a nightlight which dimly illuminated the expanse. Although he saw no one, there was possibly a night watchman inside napping. Across the way several large aluminum storage buildings glowed dimly. And toward the far end were groups of power boats on trailers, some garbage trucks, assorted maintenance trucks, and a set of private gas pumps.

He made his way to that end, keeping in the

shadows, looking often at the small lighted shack, and scanning the edges of the lot for any movement. National Park Service maintenance crews would be off duty for Saturday, Sunday, and Monday of the holiday weekend. And even after that no one might notice the missing government plates for some time. He stepped behind a large vehicle and using his tools he removed the license plate.

He took the rear plates from two different trucks because they would both be less obvious to anyone walking in the lot during the next days. No one was likely to check his vehicle to make sure that the front and rear plates matched each other. It took only a minute. Then he pulled out the tail of his shirt, stuck the plates inside and under his belt, and tucked his shirt back in to cover them. Another job well done, he congratulated himself.

From the distance, out of sight, he heard laughter and guitar music. Someone started singing "Michael, Row the Boat Ashore," and some other voices joined in. There was a campground down the hill and through the trees. And there were some employee dorms over that way too, also hidden by the slope. He walked out quickly, away from the sounds.

It was only after he was past the white shed, out of the light and onto the small dark roadway that he realized he had been hunched, crouched, condensed both outside and in. Now he straightened up by stages, taking deeper breaths and longer strides as he felt the relief which came with relaxation.

"Just a minute there!" a voice slammed from somewhere behind him.

Norman froze, his pits instantly wet. A cold

flash went down his back until it joined with the metallic unpleasantness of the license plates against his skin, suddenly a telltale hump which only others could see. He was just a short way out of the lot and his eyes had not yet adjusted to the dark.

"What? Who's there?" he called helplessly into the blackness. His legs trembled with the urge to run.

"What are you doing here?" the voice demanded, purposely, Norman felt, not identifying or locating itself, leaving him to flounder in the darkness. The politics of power.

"Hi," Norman countered as boyishly and unpowerfully as he could, but also not answering. "Which way did you come from? Did you see a moose around here?"

"Don't you know this is a restricted area?"

Now Norman could make out a huge figure at the edge of the trees. There was a path heading in the direction of the employee dormitories. The man wasn't in uniform, but that didn't mean anything at this hour of the night. When he realized he was no longer aided by invisibility, the man walked forward, even his posture conveying something hard and dominating.

"You know, it was so dark I didn't notice a thing. Actually I've been tracking a moose." He lowered his voice in excitement, as if they might inadvertently flush a timid animal from under some bush where it was hiding nearby. "I was pretty sure I saw it through the trees from the road. We're leaving tomorrow and I still haven't seen one. And I said to myself, that's what this place is all about, right? So here's my big chance. I doubled back and followed him down the road. And I walked and he walked. And I walked and he walked. And I thought to myself, pretty soon he'll get tired from all this walking and have to stop and rest. Then I'll go up and surprise him and take his picture. Oh, hell!" He looked around in disgust. "Do you know I forgot my camera?" He peered up at the man standing implacably before him. "Do you work here?"

"It's my special job to make sure people like you don't find any moose," the man said curtly. Ryner didn't specify he was a ranger. This was just the kind of turkey who would write a whining letter if he didn't like someone's tone of voice. It would have served him right if he had found a moose in the night woods. Ryner pictured with satisfaction the puddle of bloody pulp which might result from such a meeting.

"Well, I'm sorry if I did anything wrong," Norman whined. "How do I get out of here?"

"This is the way out," Ryner commanded.

Norman sidled nervously by him, staying out of reach, not turning away completely until he felt that the darkness obscured him, and the license plates he had pilfered.

Ryner watched until he was gone. Creep, he thought, and snorted, hawking his phlegm on the ground. His stomach was tight, as it so often was after these encounters, and he wasn't even sure if the man irritated him that much or if he had just tapped into the pool of subterranean rage which already lay there, waiting.

It was dealing wtih the public. It wore pretty thin after a while, trying to be Larry Goodguy all the time. Especially when over 90 percent of them were jerks, simps, or weirdos. At moments like this he sensed how close to his limit he was getting. This shit, and hanging out in the woods, had been all right when he was younger, but it had been going on for nine or ten years now. He thought he should have had a good desk by this time, with some better bucks and some expenses to round out the corners a bit. But they were hot for affirmative hiring just then. And they were putting women and all the colored into the better slots, plugging up the career ladder for who knew how many years. With ten years already invested it was hard to change. But it was getting harder and harder for him to watch his mouth, to play the game. And all the time wondering if he wasn't just heading down some blind alley.

Norman hurried along, hoping that was the way everyone walked through the woods at night. He resisted the urge to look back until he came to the main road. Then before crossing, he made a show of checking the dark for traffic and no one seemed to be behind him.

It was overcast now. Just lightly, but still no moon visible. He had always thought of the moon as steady and reliable, predictably overhead in the night sky. Until he had started to keep track of it. He got in the car and started the forty-minute drive back to Jackson, his motel, and, if he had the urge, perhaps a drink and whatever amusement happened to come along with it.

Saturday 9:00 A.M.

Crossing the arid prairie of western Nevada meant hours of nothing but dry earth randomly tufted with silvery gray sagebrush. Under the bright moon it had become a dreamscape, swept free of thought. Alice had been able to lean forward with her elbows on the wheel, point down the highway which was straight for a hundred miles at a stretch, and slide, hour after hour, without moving, as effortlessly as sitting on a conveyor. The sunrise hours had been beautiful too, the air still cool and amazingly clear. The stream she directed from the vent window to her cheek, to make sure she stayed awake, reminded her of mountain water. The oblique light shaded each contour of the land and emphasized it, rather than its essential flatness.

But approaching midmorning the sun was higher and hotter. The air rapidly lost its thirst-quenching quality and seemed instead a bit stale and lacking in oxygen. The land seemed to flatten out too and looked harsher, the same unpleasant feeling she got from a room with a naked bulb hanging overhead. The horizon was blocked by a ridge of rock. And in a saddle on that ridge sat the town of Wendover and the Utah border. On an earlier trip she remembered how she had seen that ridge and

37

hoped it represented relief, a change in elevation, in climate, in scenery. But what the ridge really was was a preview of hell. From its crest you could suddenly see the dazzling expanse of the Great Salt Lake Desert, unnaturally flat and hard-packed, stinging gray white in the full force of the sun.

That was when Ruth awoke, confused, her face crumpled like a piece of unwanted mail. "Where are we?"

The van was hot and Alice could see sweat on her neck. "About two hours from Salt Lake City."

"Want me to drive for a while?"

"You'd better wake up first."

"I could use some coffee." Ruth stretched and then made a face and stuck out her tongue. "My mouth tastes terrible." She ran long fingers through her clumps of damp curls to loosen them.

"We just passed the last coffee for two hours. Try a mint." She handed one back and Ruth took it while climbing up to sit next to her.

"You look a lot better than me and you didn't sleep at all."

"Sometimes that works better."

"Look, I have an idea. Instead of going to all this trouble, why don't we just patent this new discovery: the less you sleep the better you look. It could be a new beauty secret. Sleeping, contrary to popular belief, makes you old and tired. Do you see what I mean?"

"Exactly. Do you think you could hand me the water bottle and fix me a little sandwich? I haven't eaten anything while you've been busy sleeping and getting old and ugly." She took a long thirsty drink from the bottle Ruth handed her, but it didn't satisfy. She realized that her thirst was more for a tree and some shade. "There was a beautiful moon last night. Almost full."

"Great," Ruth replied, busy slicing cheese off a hunk that was getting runny on the outside from the heat. "No fog out here, I bet."

"About seven hours to Norman."

"Yep."

"Do you ever wonder if we might go through this whole thing and then when we're all done there's no sign of Norman? I mean maybe he just forgets, or takes off on some whim. Or changes his mind again, or something?"

Ruth looked up seriously, setting the cheese in her lap and giving Alice her full attention. "I wouldn't worry about Norman," she replied evenly.

"You mean I should worry about myself?"

"I don't think you have to worry about any of us. If I did I wouldn't be here. And I particularly think you don't have to worry about Norman. I know how he seems. Or how he *is,* sometimes. But he knows when to get down to business. Really. I knew Norman when he was straight, and married, and just out of the service, poor thing. He was nothing but business then. But just because he's learned how to fool around and get a little flippy doesn't mean he won't do what he has to."

They rode in silence. "You're right," Alice admitted after a moment. "I've been wondering how you and Norman would hold up. And it's probably really me. I keep wondering how I'll actually feel."

"That's all you talk about." Ruth waved her hands in aggravation. "I can't see why you would do this for anything but the most practical reasons. Cold hard cash, for instance. Twenty-five to forty thousand apiece. And what you could do with it.

That much money at one time can change your life forever, if you handle it right. But to do it for feeling seems . . . irresponsible. It doesn't seem like enough of a reason. And why would you even want to feel a thing like that? I know damn well it'll feel awful. I know I'll worry all the time until we do it. I'll worry while we're doing it. And I'll worry all the time we're getting away. I don't expect to even *begin* to feel good until it's completely over and I know we're all right."

"But it's not just a question of feeling *good*. It has to do with just feeling, period," Alice countered. "Even the danger. It makes me feel different. It makes me try harder. It makes me see what I can really do, when I have to. That's something I can never know until it happens. All the thinking about it, all the figuring out what I'm like and what I would do in this situation or that one, that's all bullshit, actually. I can never really know if I don't try it."

Ruth didn't reply. It reminded her of the sky-diving. One day Alice had left early and mysteriously. When she came back that afternoon she looked gray-faced and subdued. She finally explained that she had sneaked off for a skydiving package, one full day of lessons culminating in a jump. She had not, at the last minute, been able to jump. All her will had not been enough to overcome her essential terror, and she had felt crushed by what she considered a defeat. The compulsive self-testing of the self-doubting person, Ruth had thought in the privacy of her own head. She had never said that to Alice, sweet, quiet little Alice who looked like the last person in the world to be absorbed by such macho straining. So in their whole scheme Alice was a big question mark. But she refused to let herself worry about it. Weren't they all question marks until they had done it? Alice was quite right about that.

"I'm a fine one to talk about irresponsibility," Ruth offered after a minute. "Me with a three-year-old. . . . Well, I've been over that too many times already. Any day I could get hit by a car, or something. And I can't see what kind of mother I'd be if I spent the rest of my life working at the Basket and *hoping* I *would* be hit by a car." She frowned as she remembered Tisket: The Yellow Basket Boutique on Polk Street where she sold clothes and accessories.

Heat mirages, in the form of puddles on the road which disappeared without a splash as they charged them, had been appearing consistently for about an hour. So when they saw the huge pool glittering for miles along the right of the road, they rode alongside it for fifteen minutes before realizing that it really was water. Intolerably brackish and salty, but a real lake alongside the road. Perhaps it was the barrenness around them which made them think about their lives at that moment.

Not that life in the present was barren for her, thought Alice. At least she and Ruth seemed to know each other. The proof was that they were comfortable in the quiet. And when they did feel the need they could sit down over two, three cups of coffee and go over anything that needed to be said from beginning to end and have it done with.

No, it was the past where her soul still wandered like a pilgrim in the desert. And it was her father, Father the God, who still marred the quiet, speaking down from a great height. She hadn't seen

him in years, but he was still with her, still dis-
satisfied, and she spent great portions of her energy
answering him, wrestling with ancient command-
ments, seeking in the dusty archaeology of their
arguments to make things come out right.

For where she and Ruth felt they could demand
nothing from each other, had to respect their dif-
ferences, her father had wanted a great deal.
Together they had shut out her mother, pushed
her into the distance until she was little noticed.
Her father had taken her everywhere, camping
and hiking, ball games and track meets, woodshop
and model planes. It was fun, and not fun. There
was an urgency about it all, to cram it in, instilling
a curiosity which became almost driven, a com-
pulsion to experience and experiment. Looking
back now she suspected sadly that he was really an
unhappy and frustrated man, someone who had
demanded more from himself than he thought he
could deliver. Someone who wanted a partner to
share his burden, to carry on that endless, hopeless
quest.

He had both won and lost. She had torn away
from him, but he still had her, and in a deep and
unpleasant sense she was still his, still not enough
her own person. It seemed to happen abruptly,
unexpected by anyone, an enormous wrench to all
the lives concerned. When she became a teenager
her friends began to experiment with new free-
doms, going off on overnight hikes with boys. Her
father seemed suddenly to realize for the first time
that he had sired a daughter, not a son. And she
was behaving like a boy, independent, going where
she wished, coming home when she wanted, and

seeming to feel it was natural and her right. He was startled and tried quickly to correct his fifteen-year "mistake," tried to institute the discipline he felt was lacking. Tried to make her act her age and sex, like any normal person.

After several years of insane fighting she ran away and had been on her own ever since. He had trained her well. She was adaptable and although afraid at first she more than survived. She lived with groups and alone. She put herself through a year of college, and flunked out. From their point of view. From hers, *it* had flunked, failed *her* test. School was much overglorified, just another business which profited from everyone's gullibility. She worked odd jobs in places she liked. She worked as a counselor with children at summer camps. She walked dogs and watered plants for people on vacation. And the summer just two years before, Alice had been a waitress in hiking country, at Jackson Lake Lodge at the edge of the magnificent Teton Mountains in Wyoming. And now she was heading back there once again.

"It's funny, how one thing leads to another," Ruth cut into her thoughts. "There I was, bored out of my mind with sales work. It seems like it took the pain of absolute boredom to wake me up to the horrors of absolute freedom. You can really do anything you want, if you decide to." She gave a little laugh. "Sometimes I wish you couldn't."

"That's because you're getting old," Alice mocked. She ignored the face Ruth made. "I don't have it figured out in any clear way. I trust feelings. It's having the courage to follow them that's the challenge." She looked worried but she brushed away whatever she had been thinking about and smiled at her friend. "But that's no problem. This will be a good challenge," she said cheerfully and she patted her friend's leg for a moment. "Do you want to drive while I eat that sandwich?" she asked.

Saturday 3:30 P.M.

The town is just "Jackson," not Jackson Hole. "Hole" is an old trappers' term for a flat valley walled in by mountains. The Hole is the lush northern valley five to ten miles across and more than fifty miles north to south starting by Jackson but forming the floor to Grand Teton National Park, and then running on up to Yellowstone. The Snake River coils through it, gathering melted snow and glacier runoff into white-water rapids in the early part of the year, braiding and twisting strands around sandbars and islands before knotting again in narrow rock canyons.

The grassy plain on the eastern side of the valley provides grazing for elk. The ancient migratory route is now a refuge. And moose, standing heads higher than horses, wander undisturbed in the western part of the valley, browsing in the reeds and grasses of the marshy hollows. The elk are shy, clever, and difficult to approach. Even at a distance, though, they are graceful. The awkward moose, on the other hand, are left alone because they are unpredictable and often nasty. Migrating songbirds, ducks, and geese are in the air and on the water. Huge ravens, eagles, ospreys, and many hawks are overhead. More difficult to see but still thriving are beaver, coyote, black bear, porcupine, and muskrat. Silent float trips down the Snake on large rubber rafts, early in the morning or at dusk, are popular with visitors who want to see the wildlife from a close but still safe vantage point.

Jackson is a small town in the midst of a tourist boom. It is rapidly being restored in neo-frontier western, chic little shops with false wooden fronts. It is a pleasant place except for the unbearable crowding during the season: Memorial Day through Labor Day weekends. The two main roads cross at the center of town, by a green mall fringed on all four sides with parked recreation vehicles and out-of-state automobiles. The square is inhabited by sparrows who have found a unique niche in the complex modern ecology: as soon as a truck or car noses into a parking stall they flock to the radiator grille to feast on the squashed bugs. The mall was full of loungers and the town was bustling.

"My God!" was Ruth's first comment after they wedged in between a Winnebago and a Wagoneer and finally silenced the engine. Her lip was drawn up as if she smelled something bad. At the entrance to the small park was a ten-foot-high arch of hundreds of interesting elk antlers. "They must have slaughtered whole herds just to build that."

"Everyone thinks that at first," Alice laughed. "And the funny thing is they're probably the Chamber of Commerce's pride and joy. But those are all no-deposit discards. The Boy Scouts pick them up in the woods every spring. They auction them off each year to raise money. People come from as far as Japan to buy them. Use them in aphrodisiacs, I read."

"They just grow those things for a season and then drop them off?"

"Apparently." They walked around in circles, stretching arms back and kicking legs with little jerks to shake out the kinks. Directly across the street was the Cowboy Bar. They stood for another minute, hands on hips, letting the sense of movement fade, and then they crossed the street.

The bar was a cavern, enormously deep, and dark. It had been a casino at one time. Now it was packed with small round tables and as many free-floating chairs as the room could hold. It was almost a third full of drinkers savoring the last weekend of the season. In a few hours, when the country-and-western bands started, all the seats and most of the floor would be taken.

A few wranglers at the bar watched the women as they paused inside to let their eyes become used to the dark. Alice scanned the area as deeply as she could penetrate it. "It doesn't look like he's here yet," she said, starting to move toward the back for a more complete check. "But we're half an hour early," she reassured herself.

Ruth slid away from her and began slipping between the packed tables. A man was sitting alone in the middle with a bottle of beer and a shot before him. He had short, almost crew-cut, dusty brown hair and a trimmed brush mustache. He wore a red and black plaid lumberjack shirt over a navy turtleneck, real jeans, and a pair of hiking boots. His eyes were covered by sunglasses and he continued to stare expressionlessly ahead when she stopped by the table.

"Hi, Butch," she said affectionately.

He smiled up at her. "Then you like it? I wanted to see if you could pick me out."

"You look great. Your mother dressed you marvelously today. And I especially like that mustache."

"Why thank you. And here's little Alice. Did you think some strange lumberjack was picking up your friend?"

"Hello, Norman. How are you?"

"I'm fine and everything here is fine. I thought I'd better tell you that right off since you both look so tense and tired. You made good time. Have a good trip?" He signaled a waitress with three fingers and a point at his beer bottle. The waitresses were all dressed in tight black slacks and leotards, like a Broadway chorus-line version of the Hollywood version of the gunfighter.

"I'm fine," Alice told him, trying to wave off the beer put in front of her.

"You don't have to drink it, for God's sake," he assured her with exasperation. "This is a bar. If you don't have a drink you become conspicuous."

"What's that?" Ruth asked, pointing at the shot glass.

"Tequila."

"Is it camouflage or did you have some other use for it?" she asked a bit stiffly, responding, even without wanting to, to Alice's disapproval.

"After a hard day's work *I* like to relax. *You* may do as you like," he returned just as formally, warning her a bit with his voice.

"All right. What have you been doing?"

He leaned forward conspiratorially, sliding his sunglasses down on his nose so he could look at them directly with his pale gray eyes. "Everything is cool. I just got back from the park an hour ago myself. I was up there last night and again most of today. Then I dropped in here to admire the local flora and fauna. The raft is all set. I got the name tags and they're back at the motel. That makes you honored guests of Jackson Lake Lodge. The times worked out fine, Alice. You were very close. I clocked all of the points, twice, down to the second. No change in the guard schedule. I verified the floor plan. . . ." He stared into space, mentally checking off his list. "And that's it. Right?"

"I can't think of anything else," Ruth admitted.

"License plates! I got 'em."

"Great."

"Well, you two look awful. Do you want to go right back to the motel and crash, or do you want to finish your beer first?"

Ruth looked across the table at Alice. "I'm tired, but I'd like to just sit here and relax awhile before I go to sleep. How about you?" Alice shrugged. Ruth took a sip of her beer and looked around.

The open beams and posts of the bar were built of a strange bumpy wood. A sign on a rafter explained cheerfully that these wood tumors were still being studied by agricultural experts to determine the cause of the growths. The long bar, running almost the length of one wall, showed the improvement Alice had told her to expect. All the barstools had been replaced with real saddles and saddle blankets. The wranglers were sad, Alice had told her. They had been reduced, in modern times, to guiding tourists in dusty mobs along trails the tired old horses could have as easily completed without them. And now, almost caricatures of themselves, several sat on saddles turned into barstools, at no inconsiderable expense, to provide a western flavor.

Ruth finished half her beer before she wanted to go. Even Alice had taken a sip, more as a peace offering to Norman, and then offered him the rest of hers. They piled into the van and drove a few blocks to the Utopia Motel. It consisted of a dozen simple log cabins around the standard horseshoe gravel driveway.

"Park next to the station wagon," he pointed.

"Well, that looks good," Ruth approved, checking out the pink foxtail flying from the antenna and the large foam dice hanging on the rearview mirror. "The contact paper seems to be holding up well."

"Everything is just fine," he reassured them again, as if he were gradually winning an argument.

It was a simple, clean room with a bit of pine furniture which had been scalloped around the edges to give it a whittled effect. They were blocks from the highway and the center of town so it was quiet. The clean bed made their eyes water. "How about you?" Ruth asked.

"My room is right next door," he replied.

"So you'll be right next door?"

"Ah, not exactly. I was going to drop over to Idaho Falls, just over the hill, for a little trick or treat. The directory lists a bar called the White Swallow I want to check out."

"Tonight?" Alice almost wailed, losing control of her voice in her fatigue.

"Aren't you rushing the season a little?" Ruth challenged.

"For me, honey, it's always open season," he

replied, patting the ring of keys that hung from his belt. "Our agreement, as I remember it, was to work together. I don't remember ever promising not to play."

"Okay, Norman. It's just that tomorrow is very important," Ruth acquiesced. "Remember, we need you."

"I'll be good, mother. We leave at eight sharp."

"I certainly hope to see you before then! We have plenty to do."

"Never fear."

Ruth walked him out, hung the "Do Not Disturb" sign on the door, and then locked it. Alice had flopped on the bed with all her clothing on, slumped in a pile which could have been sobbing or just exhausted collapse. "Go to sleep, baby," Ruth crooned softly to her, coming over to rub the back of her neck. "You haven't slept in two days. You'll be okay after you rest up. Do you hear me?" she asked. Alice nodded agreement and mumbled something indistinguishable except for its sad, cranky tone.

Sunday 11:00 A.M.

The maid waited a minute and then knocked again, firmly. She had skipped the cabin because of the "Do Not Disturb" sign when she first came around at nine. But now that room was the only thing keeping her from ending her shift and going home. She could hear some noises from inside, so at least they were alive. She had a fear that someday she would open a door and find a mutilated body tied spread-eagled on the bed. It wouldn't be today. The door opened only a crack and she could see one sleepy eye and a bit of straight black hair.

"What is it?"

"I have to do your room."

"We don't need it today. Could you come back later? Or better, just wait until tomorrow. We're tired and we want to sleep."

"I could give you partial service," she offered, trying not to sound too eager. For reasons she couldn't quite understand, people were usually annoyed when she looked pleased at getting out of some work.

"What's that?"

"I could give you fresh towels now. Then I'd get the room tomorrow."

"That would be fine," Alice assured her, and

52

accepted the towels through the narrow opening, still keeping herself concealed behind the door.

"Do you want me to take the towels for our friend next door?" she asked.

"Oh, I did his room already. No problem. He didn't sleep there last night."

"He wasn't there?"

"If he slept there he sure didn't use the bed." The girl smiled at her little joke.

"Thank you," Alice said, started to close the door, and changed her mind. "Could you tell me something? How far is it to Idaho Falls?"

"I don't know the miles, but people here do it in a little over two hours. If they hurry. And if they don't go off the road or hit anything."

"What do you mean by that?"

"Well, you know. It's a mountain road."

Alice thanked her and closed the door quietly. She sat on the small scatter rug in the middle of the floor and immediately began to alternate breathing and stretching exercises.

"What's the matter?" Ruth asked in a muffled voice from the bed. Alice continued to work without answering. "I said, what's the matter?" Ruth asked again, waking up and lifting herself onto one elbow so she could see her friend on the floor.

"Nothing."

"You only do yoga when you're upset. Now what's the matter?"

"That's not true. I do yoga almost every day. And Norman didn't come back last night. I know he's a really old friend of yours and everything is okay so there's no need to discuss it."

Ruth made a face for her own benefit. "How are you feeling?"

"Okay."

"I mean your breathing. Can you tell if you're acclimatized? Did spending the night here help any?"

"I think it's all right. I can't tell for sure just doing this, but I feel fine. We'll be okay."

"I don't really think there's anything to worry about. With Norman, I mean. I've known him to sometimes trick every night for weeks and never be late for work in the morning."

"Fine. Really. I know everything will be just all right."

"Do you feel like getting some breakfast then?"

"Not right now. My stomach's too upset." She looked up at Ruth and one little laugh popped out of her like a bubble.

Sunday 7:00 P.M.

For the third time that hour Ruth put down the visitors' pamphlet she was trying to read and stepped quickly to the window when she heard a car on the gravel. "It's Norman," she announced with relief, holding the stiff little curtain to one side so she could peek out. "Oh, my God!"

"What is it?" Alice demanded. She hopped over to the window. "Jesus, I knew it," she said with a certain satisfaction. Norman was getting out of the green wood-paneled station wagon with a strange dog. They watched silently as he walked it around the parking lot a bit to see if it had to pee, and then locked it back in the wagon.

Norman came in smiling and pleasant, apparently unprepared for his reception. "What's with that dog, Norman?" Ruth demanded without even saying hello. "This is too late to start fooling around!"

He ignored that. "I found it tied to a fire hydrant right outside the bar," he explained agreeably. "One look and I knew it was just what I needed to complete my outfit." To him it was clearly a sign of his improvisational genius. To the women it was an unexpected factor at a time when even the known factors were barely tolerable.

"Norman, we had this all planned out!"

"Well, I just improved the plans!"

"How are we going to get rid of that dog?" Alice interjected. "Just run that down to me quickly, if you'd please."

"No problem," he insisted. "I have that all figured out."

The two women stared at each other, their faces dark with all the congested feelings which they were trying to keep from expressing.

"Look!" Norman was finally growing impatient too. "It's my job to do the lobby. You want me to steal the show? I'll do it." His voice was growing stiff with uncompromising finality. "I don't tell you how to hike, so don't you tell me how to camp." Even in the midst of that scene he couldn't completely ignore the humor in the remark and his mouth twisted, in spite of himself, into a small, ironic smile. Alice saw it and rolled her eyes as if it were the last straw.

Ruth stepped in between them quickly. "Okay, Norman, okay. There's no reason for us to fight about this. I'm sure you know what you're doing. So we're just going to leave your part to you, like you say. We'll leave it to you and we'll just count on you to take care of your end of it. And that's that," she said without any feeling that the matter was really finished. "We'll just take your word, and we'll all do our parts and everything will be all right."

"I'm going into the bathroom to get ready," Alice announced from the back of the room. "You two decide what you want to do. I don't care what

it is. Just decide something, for Christ's sake."
She wheeled into the little room and slammed the
door.

"Don't worry, everything is okay, Alice," Ruth
called after her. "No problem. It's okay," she repeated more softly, but sarcastically, glaring at
Norman. When she heard the water begin to run
she turned to him in exasperation. "Norman, what
are you doing?"

His answer was to stare her down coldly, his
head tilted back just a bit.

"Okay, okay. Do what you want," she acquiesced, turning away from him.

Norman went quickly to his cabin next door.
The pressure was on him now, not to hold them
up, not to ruin everything. He began his baroque
preparations with as much haste as he could control.

Ruth wasn't going to think about it, she decided.
She wasn't going to think about anything for a
while, if she could manage it. The whole idea
seemed clearly crazy now, so what good could
thinking do? She knew there wasn't one of them
who wouldn't be relieved if something happened
to stop them, some uncontrollable outside force
which was beyond anyone's responsibility. But all
the energy and preparation that had gone into
this, all the innocent enthusiasm of their earlier
planning, the thin, questionable arguments they
had used to convince themselves in the first place,
had all combined to establish a momentum which
none of them seemed to have the courage or the
strength to resist. Even Alice who was frightened
close to hysteria. Even Norman who had to sneak
off for drinking and whoring on the very eve of

their action just to settle himself down. Even herself who since morning had felt like she was slipping out of control down a long, smooth gray tunnel, a cross between a cannon barrel and a sewer main, sliding deeper and darker into something that seemed hopeless and joyless forever.

Sunday 8:05 P.M.

Ready at last, they huddled together just inside the door, peering out into the now darkening parking lot to make sure there was no one about to see them. Then they left quickly and in a single continuous motion the women were in the wagon and Norman was seated in the van. They started engines almost simultaneously and pulled slowly out onto the road, Norman leading and Ruth trailing him. On the dashboard of the wagon was a legal-size pad of yellow paper with Norman's handwriting. "Jackson-Moose, 15 min. at 50 mph," the first entry said. Ruth checked the speedometer warily with a flick of her eyes. They were doing just over sixty. They were running a few minutes late and Norman was trying to make up the time. They were exceeding the speed limit, but it would probably be all right.

Of course, if they were stopped by a ranger patrol car now it might mean the end of the whole thing. She checked the rearview mirror for a flashing red-top behind them. There was nothing. Was she hoping, she wondered? Well, whatever happened would happen, she decided, philosophical in the absence of better alternatives.

There was almost no transition. It was a small

town and ended abruptly. The elk refuge spread out flatly on the right—water, bog, and plain— all the way to the Gros Ventre Range and the Teton National Forest. Not as showy as the Tetons, still invisible on the left, the opposite wall of the valley. Norman had told them that all the local people hiked and camped there during the summer, enjoying the relative solitude, while thousands upon thousands of tourists packed into the dramatic Tetons. All this and I've never even seen them, Ruth was thinking, remembering the brochures with their photos of the mountains in every season. They should be right along here somewhere, she decided.

Alice had been staring ahead, lost in the future, her face serious and determined as she rode. Ruth expected a silent trip in. It was a serious time for them all.

She was surprised when Alice suddenly spoke. "There," she said simply as they came out of a small draw, about three miles from town.

The earth bank some fifteen feet higher than the car on the left began to fall away and the abrupt faulted peaks of the Tetons, the jagged stone pickets partly whitewashed in snow, appeared in the dusk. Ruth was prepared to be impressed by the mountains, although she had heard such an abundance of gushing and exclaiming when people talked of them that she had held private reservations. Now she realized they had been trying vainly to transmit an experience which was essentially indescribable. She was glad there were only the two of them there. On a crowded tour bus she would have felt inhibited. But now she surrendered, letting herself give in to a thrill which was broader and less personal than sex, but in no way inferior to it. Alice felt it too, she knew. Alice loved the mountains.

They rode in silence for several minutes, the hill continuing to drop on the left and the mountains continuing to rise, until they were at their full height, over thirteen thousand feet, a sudden icy wall perpendicular to the flat plain which stretched between them. "The French trappers called them the Trois Tetons. That means the three breasts," Alice announced, proud of her acquaintanceship with them. "That somehow seems appropriate."

"Then Grand Teton, the big one, means Big Tit," Ruth said with satisfaction. They passed the turnoff to the Jackson Hole Country Club. And a few miles further, the road to the airport, a single runway parallel to the mountain range. And finally they came to Moose Junction and turned left.

Ahead were the park headquarters and ranger station. Outside, blocking the road, were the tollbooths where the entrance permits were sold. Large steel guardrails, extending out like the bows of boats, protruded in either direction, indicating the lanes and protecting the little tollhouses from ramming. Several years before, someone had come through late at night, after the booths were closed, and drunkenly leveled one of them with his new pickup. But Norman turned right before he came to them and took a small road toward the river for a few hundred yards. This was a parking lot and a river access for some of the float trips.

A group of about twenty visitors was standing in the lot talking quietly. The last trip of the day was often the best because so many animals came to the water at dusk. Much of the trip was in silence, or whispers, and that peacefulness extended for some time afterward. Only the two powerful boatmen were working energetically. They were dragging the huge rubber raft up the cement ramp which led from the river, pulling toward a flatbed trailer hooked to a small van.

Norman parked well away from them. There would be no questions about his van left in the parking lot. The women pulled the wagon right alongside and he crossed to it unnoticed. It was a relief to stand up. For just a moment the crippling pressure was off his cock and balls. Blood almost started to circulate. And then he was seated in the wagon, gritting his teeth and bearing the pain again.

Ruth returned the wagon to the main road and through Moose Gate. She bought their two-dollar entrance permit from the ranger in the booth and was told it was good for Yellowstone as well, just to the north. She thanked him, and they headed silently into the park in the deepening night.

They got one glimpse of the lodge from the distance, a large brown building on a bluff overlooking the marsh and the lake. "That's it," Alice noted flatly, but it was too quick and too dark and too far to mean much to Ruth as she drove. There was no moon yet and the mountains were only an uncertain afterimage when they glimpsed them between the trees.

Sunday 8:30 P.M.

Upstairs in the lodge lecture hall the second lecture, the one on hypothermia, was finishing up. Diane, the park ranger, was pointing to slides of cadavers and saying to the audience: "It's strange, but you can tell even in photographs that these people are dead and not asleep, or even unconscious. Something is gone from them, and even the camera can see it." This one had wedged himself into a crack in a rock wall, a small hollow more than an actual cave. A damp, cold place which offered only the illusion of protection. Instead of the common lead gray or purple-gray color of death, this one had a pinkish face to indicate he died from the cold. Not as vivid as the bright pink of carbon-monoxide poisoning, but still a distinct, eerie pink.

Diane signaled Mike again for the lights. On the second floor of the lodge the lecture hall was only half-full. By this time everyone knew where the bar was.

"Hypothermia doesn't have to occur in the mountains," she said. "That is where it is most common, but it can strike almost everywhere. Victims usually succumb without even knowing it.

"Awareness is the only real protection. Awareness of the manner and of the great speed with which hypothermia can kill. But unfortunately awareness of this disorder is still quite limited. Until very recently these deaths have been attributed to 'exposure' without a real understanding of what has happened.

"Early signs may be tiredness, weakness, slowness, forgetfulness, and confusion. All normal enough on a hard hike to easily ignore. By the time the symptoms develop the individual is usually past the point of being able to recognize the danger, or do much in the way of self-help. Someone else must immediately realize what is happening and *act,* without being signaled by complaints, if the affected individual's life is to be saved. Under difficult conditions the first symptoms may occur in one to two hours, collapse may follow as soon as an hour later, and death may be only two hours behind that."

Talking about death made her think of the autopsy slides which ended the lecture. They showed the other aspect of the mountains. The evidence that survival could not be guaranteed by the park service, or by any other governmental agency.

"Hypothermia is a sickness of cooling. Cold, wet, windy conditions cause the most loss of heat, and the greatest danger. If you add to that an individual who is tired, not well nourished, or not dressed in wool, you have the critical mixture. Wool is a simple protection against hypothermia because it is the only natural fabric which insulates when wet. It is potentially a life-saving part of any mountain hiker's equipment.

"To protect the functioning of vital organs the body allows its surface to cool while maintaining a warm core. Unfortunately, soon after this the muscles just under the skin become clumsy, and then more or less inoperative. Hikers who are lucky enough to recognize the early symptoms may then find that their hands no longer function adequately to build a fire or even to zip a sleeping bag around themselves.

"And a sleeping bag alone is no cure. Treatment requires replacing the lost heat. Merely wrapping the stricken person in a sleeping bag, in blankets, or other insulation, will *not* help if the condition has advanced. Victims lose the ability to replace lost heat. It is necessary to put the suffering person in a sleeping bag naked, with a healthy hiker who is also naked. This provides body-to-body heat transfer, which is the most effective life-saving procedure under wilderness conditions.

"Perhaps we should take a look at another case." She was beginning to feel the need for a rest, and the histories were easy to read. "I'll tell you about a young couple," she said to them.

"Evelyn and Barry Wright, early twenties, recently married, good health, inexperienced hikers. They went off for a picnic hike in the mountains. The weather was warm, in the low eighties on the valley floor, and they wore light cotton clothing and had no rain gear or wind protection. They went off the trail, against regulations and without an adequate map, to climb up the narrow gorge of a glacial stream they thought was especially pretty. To enter the canyon they had to cross the stream on low rocks.

"The wind picked up as they reached a higher level and they found a natural shelter against a boulder with two trees fallen over it. There they

ate a light lunch, which was all the food they had
brought, and spent several hours relaxing." The
newlyweds had been making love, she knew, but
she felt no inclination to tell them that. "It started
to rain and they stayed several more hours in their
shelter waiting for it to stop. It became colder and
the rain turned unexpectedly to snow. Very likely
if they had remained in their shelter and built a
fire they would have managed, but they didn't
know that. Instead they descended, and at lower
levels the snow turned into rain again and they
were immediately soaked to the skin. The rain and
wind in combination chilled them to the point of
clumsiness and they had difficulty walking. When
they came to the mouth of the gorge they found
the stream so swollen by rain that they doubted
they could cross it. The rocks were covered with
rushing water now, and they were stiff and so
clumsy from the cold they were afraid of being
swept off their feet and tumbled down into the
rocky ravine.

"They began climbing back up to find shelter,
but now they were too weak to return to their original place. They crouched among some wet rocks
which blocked a portion of the winds but drew off
considerable body heat by conduction to the cold
surface. Their hands were too stiff to be useful, and,
ironically, they charred several hundred dollars of
their vacation money in a vain attempt to start a
fire. Barry had slipped into the stream several times
and soaked his feet. By evening he seemed sure
they wouldn't be rescued and didn't care. Evelyn
seemed more determined to survive and forced
herself to exercise to generate some heat, resisting
sleep as well as she could. Next morning a rescue

sweep found them and was able to rewarm Evelyn enough to get her down. Barry had stopped breathing only a short time before they were found. Besides Evelyn's light wool sweater and greater will to live, she had the additional advantage of being a woman. The thicker layer of underskin fat gives women a significant advantage in resisting cold."

She liked to end that way, even though she seriously doubted that her small moral was taken to heart. When Mike finished the stack of slides Diane closed by again extending them a welcome on behalf of the park service and the lodge. She assured them that she, or any ranger, would be available for discussion or to answer questions. Then she instinctively braced herself a bit. She was more than used to it, of course. But still her eyes narrowed in tense appraisal as she looked out over the group.

Mike was handsome in his ranger uniform, walking up from the rear with a bounding, arm-swinging step. Nineteen and healthy, and awed by the fact that as soon as he had put on the uniform, people, or at least tourists, had suddenly begun to take him seriously. And now he was stopped several times as he crossed the floor with questions about Diane's lecture.

A man in uniform looks like the real thing, she thought. We're conditioned that way. It's an automatic, unthinking response for most people. No one came up to ask her anything. Tourists whom she did talk to sometimes admitted that they thought she was some type of naturalist-volunteer, a wildlife candy striper of some sort, doing good in the woods.

"Hi, hon," she said to her nephew as he finally approached. She kept the edge out of her voice. It wasn't his fault. "It felt like it went pretty well."

"The lecture was great," he assured her. "But those slides are *wretched!*"

Sunday 8:41 P.M.

When they finally saw the lodge again it was sudden and they came right up to it. Quite large and square, made of some brown stone suspiciously like tinted concrete. Even with the roof crouching low and flat it was still a massive building.

The circular drive swung under a large portico protecting the main entrance. The roof of the portico served as a deck. This evening it hosted a cocktail party and was crowded with drinkers in suits and evening dresses. Ruth pulled into the nearest lot, found a space, and parked.

"You all right?" Ruth asked Alice.

"Sure," she answered, pushing her glasses up tighter with a jerky little shove.

"My balls are killing me," griped Norman.

"A few minutes more. Keep low in the car until we get inside. We'll go around and come in from the back terrace. If we don't see anything weird we'll give you a wave in the lobby. And it's 'go' from that minute. Okay, give us three minutes, from now!"

Norman was squirming, trying to readjust his clothing.

"Look at your watch, Norman! Three minutes from now." She reached across and patted him on the leg. Then she opened the door and called to Alice, "C'mon," and got quickly out.

By the time they came to the doors several people had turned to look after them. They were two well-dressed women with large floppy summer bags who were hurrying anxiously along the back terrace. "This will not do, this will not do," Ruth intoned at the door. She put her hand on Alice's arm to stop her from rushing automatically on-ward.

"A little more slowly, a little more slowly," she chanted tensely under her breath to mark the pace for both of them. She continued in singsong, trying to look like she was engaged in animated conversation with Alice.

"Everyone dressed up so pretty. Having *good* time. We having good time too. Dressed up so fancy, walking through lounge. Down stairs to lobby!" and she tightened her grip on Alice's arm.

A lecture was breaking up and the stairs became a waterfall of bobbing heads. Some rangers brushed near, a woman and a young man, rocks to be avoided in the rapids. But they swirled safely away. Ruth forced a steady stream of chatter to keep lubricated, to keep her mind from catching on some snag.

They were just reaching the bottom of the long stairway when Norman came in, sooner than she had expected. His effect was palpable and immediate. Ruth towed Alice toward a side of the lobby into the shelter of a large pillar. From there they could watch Norman and still see down the hall-way that ran back along the right of the stairs.

Under the staircase was the door to the accounting office.

Those who were facing the main entrance looked up and stopped talking. Those standing sideways saw the others looking and turned their heads. Finally even the rest turned. It became silent, everyone realizing at the same instant and politely resuming small talk. Everyone had looked. And while most did not continue to stare, neither did anyone turn completely away.

Of course he was gorgeous. But it was his manner as much as how he actually looked. Perhaps something was subtly off-key but not easily recognizable. He radiated energy, glamour, and a confusing challenge to both the men and the women in the room.

The dog was class, a purebred Afghan. From its long aristocratic nose almost four feet of golden coat flowed to the floor. With it Norman looked like something between an opera diva and a high-class hooker. But the dog was terrified by the transformation in Norman. It crouched slightly, at the extreme end of its leash, rolling its eyes back at him. If only it wouldn't cower every time Norman twitched the long, green feather boa.

To remember how he looked he had to ignore how he felt. On the outside he was a tall redhead, statuesque in a green and white I. Magnin flowered print. But underneath he felt trussed and bound like after a major accident. Heavy adhesive crisscrossed his chest to push a fleshy cleavage above the tops of his falsies. Cock and balls were forced down between his thighs and imprisoned under a tight girdle. Even his face felt stiff and artificial. After his makeup he had sealed the paint with hair spray, careful not to lacquer his eyes shut. But he looked beautiful. He felt outrageous, and he was ready to go. "Craig Russell, eat your heart out!" he fluffed.

A door closed and Ruth turned to see the security guard walk away from the accounting office. He headed to the rear of the building on the old habit of his rounds. Next would come visits at the bakery, laundry, butcher shop, and loading platform, a cycle that would lead him through the building and then back here. "Forty-five minutes from *now*," Ruth said, noting precisely when the circuit started.

Ruth stepped clear of the post, and looking tensely at Norman, she gave one sharp nod. This is it. Her look hung on his face until she was sure she had eye contact. Norman smiled back brilliantly, theatrically, and then swirled away, dragging the dog as he went. He turned only to see the information hostess trotting right at him.

"Oh, do it good, Norman," Ruth pleaded under her breath. The two women moved to the rear along the stairs. Alice looked determined, but miserable. "Whatever will be," Ruth told herself, trying to breathe deeply and evenly.

Almost opposite the door the guard had just left was another one marked "Ladies." Alice pushed in there, going first, and without a word went down the row, checking every stall. Ruth stood at the door. When Alice gave her the nod she turned the latch to secure it. They each knelt where they were and opened their bags, intent on the drill, trying to be as smooth and quick as possible without fumbling, the point which was the beginning of panic.

Ruth dumped out the cloth sleeve and extracted the rifle stock from its concealment. She pried off the rubber butt pad. She pulled barrel, action, and clip from their compartments in the stock, laid them on the floor, and began to assemble all the parts.

God, the guns looked ugly. In fact they looked as if they had been designed with intimidation in mind, as much as functionality. Although with a gun, intimidation was a basic function. The action sloped back at an angle which reminded her of a submachine gun. The short barrel recalled the sawed-off look of shotguns she had seen in movies about bank robberies. And the molded gray Cycloac stock looked sinister even without the gun attached to it.

"We could probably just walk in with the handle and no one would question us," Alice had joked in a time that was easier and far away.

There was a sharp thunk as the door pushed forcefully inward, and hit the lock. The pieces of Alice's gun slid away from her, clattering across the tile floor. Her glasses fell with them, bouncing away among the gun parts. She waited, her head up and frozen in place like a wild animal startled in the woods. She listened to the danger before she went after the scattered pieces. Another thunk, and then a series of rattles as some determined urinator persisted, either stubborn or desperate.

"Cleaning up in here," Ruth called, almost yelling to make sure she was heard through the door. It was a strain to raise her voice and force it through tight vocal cords. There was another tentative rattle.

"There's been a little accident. Cleaning up.

We'll only be a minute. Just hold your horses."
They turned to their work again, feeling even more
feverish and harried than before.

Ruth snapped the eight-shot magazine into place
as Alice, kneeling at the other end of the wash-
room, mirrored her movements just as they had
choreographed and practiced them so many times
back home on the living room floor. They slid the
assembled guns into their bags again. The stocks
protruded now, but held up under their arms their
shawls concealed them adequately. They faced
each other. Alice looked dazed and she seemed to
be breathing shallowly.

"Alice, what happened to your glasses?" Ruth
whispered shrilly. There was a great vertical crack
through one lens. And the upper quadrant was a
mesh of fine lines.

"They fell when she shook the door." Her voice
quavered and she bit her lip.

"What are you going to do?"

"I can't wear them like this. They couldn't be
more conspicuous. I'll have to put them in my
pocket before we go out of here."

"But you can't see very far without them."

"No," Alice moaned in frustration.

"You'll be all right." Ruth patted her arm. "Our
business will be close up. Just stay near me."

Ruth took a deep breath, like before a dive from
the high board, and unlocked the door. They
walked out together, looking into the lobby to check
the action. There were two women outside, their
backs to them. Blue-white hair, expensive summer
dresses, jewelry. They were totally absorbed by the
spectacle mesmerizing guests and staff throughout

the front of the lodge, forgetting the bathroom which originally drew them there.

Norman saw but gave no signals now, except to glance at the ladies' Timex on his wrist. He was on, Ruth thought fatalistically. For the next three minutes the stage was his. They would be behind the scenes. And in *four* minutes he should be parked right outside in the wagon with the motor running. That was the plan. Now she and Alice had their own work to do.

The women crossed the hall and pushed into a room full of desks and filing cabinets. The accounting office had closed at four-thirty on Saturday, and the staff had gone for the holiday weekend. The lights were on, piles of cashiers' tapes were folded in wire baskets on each desk, everything ready for work on Tuesday. To the right was a smaller office, through a set of Dutch doors with the top hooked back for ventilation. That was the cashier's office, lined with brick.

Inside they could see the top of a bald head, delicate and pinkly pale as it floated low over the ledgers. "Did you forget something?" Allen asked absentmindedly, thinking the security guard had returned. He didn't look up for the moment, busy recording something in the huge book open before him.

The three of them were alone there. In the big office where they stood was a large walk-in safe. But no money was kept there, Alice had told her. It stored valuable records, the concern being more with fire than with theft. And at the end of the season it held the better wines and hard liquor because it was only a little pilferage from the winter crew, not actual robbery, that anyone thought about. It was the wall safe in the next room, right behind that little man, which was the real thing.

Allen raised his head.

"Oh," Ruth chirped as prettily as she could. "This isn't the ladies' room?" She smiled at him.

"No, indeed." He smiled back. "We like to think of this as the accounting office. What you're looking for is across the hall."

"Across . . . ?" Ruth started to turn one way and then the other, gesturing weakly in the direction he had indicated. She squinted as she strained to understand his instructions. Without her glasses now, Alice just stood there, quite confused. Ruth hoped deeply and sincerely that it was an act like hers.

The bald man got up politely to show her the way. She tried not to stare past him at the steel frame set into the wall, the heavy door open just as Norman said it would be Friday night at this time. Allen came toward them and opened the bottom half of the door. Ruth strained silently at him, mentally pulling him closer, step by step. Once he walked out it was all right. Now he was safely away from buzzers and alarms, away from that steel safe door which he just might, in bravery or loyalty or foolishness, suddenly slam shut before they could even decide if it was worth shooting to stop him. He reached out to take Ruth's arm and point her toward the toilets.

She pushed him off and they hoisted the guns from their bags. It was unpleasant to realize she had put that look on his face. No one had ever looked at her that way before. But his complete shock was also reassuring.

"Nothing here worth getting killed for," Ruth

warned, her voice clumsy in her mouth even though she had practiced the speech at home in her bathroom. He was a short, pale man, fringe-bald, and cowering now. He looked so much like a central casting accountant that she had a feeling of unreality, like she was watching TV instead of actually doing it. Something in her wanted to sit down and see what happened next. She had to force herself to move, leaving Alice to cover the man while she walked quickly around him to look in the safe. The accountant didn't look like he could be trouble. He hardly seemed to exist in the real world, wherever that was now.

But the strange sound behind her made her twist suddenly back. It was a grunt and a gurgle, a stifled sound, and she couldn't tell which of them had made it. The man had grabbed Alice's gun barrel and was pulling it in both hands. The muzzle was pointed right at his stomach and she shuddered to think what would happen if Alice touched the trigger. They had both braced their feet and were tugging on it. Like two children about to break into a self-righteous argument which she as the mother would be required to settle. His face had gone red now and Alice's was pale. Ruth scrambled back and hit him a slapping blow with the side of her gun stock, catching him on a shiny spot where his forehead merged with his temple. He fell backward onto his can and Ruth steadied her gun between his eyes. She knew he wouldn't move. She could see that she had command over him and he would do exactly what she said.

Without even glancing at her, Ruth knew Alice was terrified and almost nonfunctional. But hitting the man had had exactly the opposite effect on her. The action had freed her from the unreality. We're really doing it, she realized and exulted that there was finally no way out, back, around, under —any way but straight on through. For her it had now entered the realm of athletics, and she understood in her guts, without the equivocation of her mind, that she should move strongly and follow through smoothly.

"On your stomach. Put your hands behind your back," she ordered, enjoying the impatience in her voice, profoundly relieved by having the chance to act. "Keep your gun pointed right here," she ordered Alice, tapping the man's head sharply with her rifle barrel just in front of his ear. He winced at the contact and shut his eyes in fear. Her command was more for his benefit than Alice's. Neither of them could fire that accurately after a bare two hours' practice in a deserted Sierra canyon. And she had no idea if Alice could act even if it were necessary now.

Ruth scooped the roll of tape from her bag and wrapped his wrists together. Then his ankles. She took a clean sock from the bag and pushed it into his mouth. He opened it obligingly. Then she put tape across that to hold it in.

"Can you breathe all right?" she asked, letting her voice soften now that he was no danger. Ruth put her gun on the floor, turned his head gently in both her hands, and looked into his eyes. He nodded. "Good. Just relax now and you'll be fine," and she patted him comfortingly on his back. She checked her watch but it made no sense. She was too impatient to look at it long enough for it to register. She was hyper, she realized, but for God's sake, how else could you be at a time like this? The hell with the time. They would just have to do it and see what happened. So much for clockwork split-second timing.

Alice was standing over the man, watching the lump rise on his head. There was a scrape but no blood showing yet. He would be all right. If Alice gets hysterical what can I do? All that came to mind was the standard slap in the face. She only knew that from movies and had no idea if it was worth a damn in real life. And it would certainly be a strange time for them to start hitting each other.

"Come here and help me load," she commanded as she walked to the safe. Alice followed her, some of the color starting to return to her face.

They went to the wall safe, trusting that the man on the floor couldn't see them and wouldn't try anything. And besides, it was feeling late to Ruth and she thought they should go as fast as they could now. They packed their bags with banded bills, appalled at how rapidly the weight and bulk accumulated. Ruth was trying to sort, to pick the bundles of largest denomination. Alice seemed to be packing anything that came into her hand, but Ruth made no attempt to correct her. She was afraid she might only confuse her more. Alice started to check the drawers. The first she opened was full of rolled coins. "Leave that," Ruth told her simply. "This will have to do."

They were bent over their bags, leveling the piles of money and settling it as low as possible, when the phone rang. Their heads jerked up and they searched, as it rang again. It was on Allen's desk, where he was supposed to be working at that very moment. Ruth scurried over.

She forced her hands into Allen's armpits, difficult because his hands were taped behind him,
and dragged him clumsily behind his desk. Alice
was biting her lip again and looking as if she
might cry. Ruth cursed long dresses and high shoes
as she worked, grunting and awkward, with her
load.

The telephone kept up its regular, agonizing insistence.

"You've got to answer that phone," Ruth panted.
"Whatever they say, everything is all right and
they don't want to come in here now. Understand?"
She shook his shoulders like a bad child.

Allen nodded and the phone rang again. Ruth
grabbed the tape by one corner and yanked it off
his mouth, the sock coming with it. "Ech!" he
winced.

"Sorry," Ruth apologized. The phone rang again
and she twitched.

"We're very nervous," she warned him one last
time and yanked the phone off the hook before it
could ring again.

"Allen, where were you?" the voice demanded.

"I was busy with something," Allen gasped to
the phone that Ruth held on his face. She knelt,
her ear next to his so she could listen too. She had
pulled her gun over and was pressing it against
him as an additional warning.

"This is Gracie. Come on out to the lobby. Right
now! This is something you won't want to miss."
Her voice was enthusiastic.

"Just a minute. I'll be out in just a minute,
Gracie. Thanks for letting me know."

"Okay, but you'd better hurry."

"Right, Gracie. I'll be right out." He nodded to Ruth and she hung up the phone.

"Norman! Is Norman all right?" Alice demanded.

Ruth looked at her. "I don't know," she admitted, "I don't know what's happening out there."

"What did she want?"

"She just told him to come out and look. Let's get out of here!"

Ruth pressed the tape back over Allen's mouth. Then she hoisted his hands up behind him and taped them quickly to one of the drawer handles. It was probably uncomfortable, but she thought he would be all right. And it looked as if it would be extremely difficult for him to move.

Next they worked at wedging the guns back into the bags, now full of paper money. Forcing them in, muzzle first, was a halfway job and much of the guns including the trigger and action still stuck out.

"I can't get mine all the way in," Alice complained, looking up at Ruth for help.

"Of course not. They're full!" Ruth snapped impatiently. Then, less sharply, "Hold the bag high and make sure your shawl covers everything." She arranged it for her quickly. " 'Cause if you don't . . ." and she gave Alice a significant look.

Ruth went back and bent over the man. "You've done fine, so don't ruin it now," she told him. "We'll be in the lobby for a while. If you come out while we're there we'll have to shoot you. Nobody wants that, not even your boss, so just relax for a few minutes and everything will be okay." It sounded all right to her, but she didn't have

time to think about it. She had no recollection now
of what speech she had practiced for that moment.

They stood together at the door, wondering what
might be waiting for them on the other side.

"I won't be able to see much out there," Alice
said softly, so Allen wouldn't hear.

"You'll be okay. Just stay close," Ruth reassured. "Straight across, don't hurry, and keep the
gun covered." Ruth tried to sound matter-of-fact.
As she opened the door she had visions of the Tech-
nicolor, slow-motion, bullet-riddled deaths of Bon-
nie and Clyde.

To their surprise everyone in the lobby seemed
to be talking at once. No one paid any attention to
them. "This is the *last* place I would expect *that*
kind of a scene," someone huffed enthusiastically
as they passed quickly by. Ruth didn't care that the
guests had been so titillated by Norman's act. She
wasn't gathering reviews for later. Later was too
far in the future, too theoretical, too unreal. Now
she listened only for a shrill voice saying, "That's
them! There they go!"

The bellman saw them coming and swept the
door back, almost sucking them out into the night
with the grand and practiced movement of his arm.
He alone stared at them, his eyes bright with his
interest. It was immediately clear why. Norman
was waiting for them, pulled up right before the
door, so incongruous in his elegance, so flamboy-
ant in the wood-paneled station wagon with the
pink foxtail and foam dice. The heap of equipment
was piled darkly in the rear; they had forgotten
to cover it. And now the two conservative doctors'
wives from the Northwest, both looking dazed,
one on the verge of tears, rushed awkwardly to-

ward the back door which the gorgeous driver leaned across and opened for them. Hurried toward that remarkable dog, possibly the only Afghan in the state of Wyoming. All of that Ruth sensed and ignored. She listened only for the sharp, taloned cry that would come after them, stabbing and clutching, to pull them back, to throw them down.

And down indeed! Alice shrieked at Ruth's ear and stumbled past, her shoe tangled in her dress, grabbing Ruth's arm as she fell. Both of them almost falling but just managing to hold each other up. Ruth's dress pulled off one shoulder and Alice's bag pinwheeling out of her hand as the two women staggered helplessly at the exit.

Alice scrambled madly after the bag, down on her knees now, gathering it up in both desperate hands, miraculously intact and unspilled, the snap somehow holding. Her shawl, snagged on the gun, falling with it, disguising it for the moment. The doorman, professionally gallant, rushed forward to help, and Ruth, desperate to block his view, jumped between them and muttered fiercely, "Leave her alone! She doesn't feel good."

She pushed Alice in ahead of her and stumbled after, slamming the door on the corner of her shawl and opening it again to free it as Norman pulled away, wondering if the guns had been under or over the shawls all that time. Knowing she never, *never* would have tried any of this if she had realized how random and unplanned so many tiny and vital elements would be, how little control they had, in reality, maintained over their destinies and welfares, what an illusion their planning actually was.

As Norman swerved out of the lot Alice pulled her wig off and let her dark hair fall with relief. She rubbed the ring around her forehead where the blood had stopped on its way to her brain, letting the feeling return not only to her head but to her whole body. And then, finally released, she rested her face in the comforting of her open palms and let herself sob freely.

Ruth pulled her wig off also and then continued, automatically, to peel at the rest of her clothing. She threw her wig, panty hose, and shoes on the floor by her feet. In just four minutes she had become emotionally exhausted. She wished she could lean back and not move for hours.

"I'm so glad that's over," Alice sobbed. "I never want to do that again." She raised her face from her hands, her eyes red and a few bubbles of spit stuck to her lips, and gave Ruth a maniacal grin. "Whatever made us think we could do an awful thing like that?" she asked and began to laugh insanely.

She looked so horrible that Ruth began to laugh too. "But we did it! We did it," she laughed weakly back.

"I know. That's what's so funny!" Alice insisted. "I couldn't see a freakin' thing the whole time!"

Norman was completely serious, however. He had taken down the yellow pad from the dash and was checking the figures again: "24 min from Lodge to raft." The "24 min" was underlined twice. He slowed with a lurch to 15 mph as the road walked the top edge of the Jackson Lake dam, a few vague forms standing by the spillway below with fishing rods. Then he pressed the speedometer back exactly to the 45 mph mark, staying precisely at the limit, guiding the car along the barely familiar road in the dark.

"Are you getting ready?" They didn't answer him. "This is tight," he warned. "When we get to the place, you get out, ready or not, you understand? I'm not going to stick around and get my ass fried just because you aren't ready." He scanned the sky to the southeast. No sign of the moon yet. Everything on schedule if they didn't screw it up. He forced himself to constantly check the dark bicycle path on the right of the road. All they needed would be to hit some idiot out for a nighttime bike ride.

"Relax, Norman," Alice commanded, passing the cold cream to Ruth as she finished toweling off her makeup. She put her hands on his shoulders and gave him a little shake.

"Cut that out."

"We'll be ready, Norman. Now don't you go acting like some hysterical woman," she chided him.

"Just get started, *please*," he begged. "You've got a lot to do. The guard could come back early or that guy might get loose. . . . I really want those extra minutes. Come on, move it."

The pile of clothing grew on the floor as their bodies slowly emerged in the dark of the back seat. Ruth felt her nipples tighten and her small breasts drew up in the cold wind rushing through the open windows. It chilled her but also woke her and refreshed her and she was glad for that. She was coming back into real contact again and she was grateful. Alice stripped her halter also and Ruth glimpsed for an instant the smooth white flesh of the dark-haired woman, the tender skin that reminded her so often of a fish's belly. And then it disappeared under a cotton undershirt, soft, to cushion that skin from the fishnet underwear she pulled over it. The insulation would be there but that way the pack would not grind the coarse netting into those soft shoulders with every step.

Ruth wiggled into her own long underwear bottoms, raising her hips awkwardly in the tight space to tug them up over her butt. "Oh, hell!" she said with sudden awareness. "I think I'm getting my period."

"You're not due, are you?" Alice asked.

"It was probably the excitement."

"Do you want a Tampax?"

"They're in the pack. It's okay for now. I'll do it on the trail."

"Will you be all right?" Norman asked, concerned.

"I'll just have to be," Ruth answered him. "I don't have much choice," but her voice was sour. She didn't like this.

They pulled on wool pants. Wool, the fabric which would allow them to tolerate the snow on the ridges and in the higher passes. It was important protection, not just against general misery but against the potentially deadly cold as well. And then two pair of wool socks. Two pair, as she had learned from Alice, so one would slip within the other and spare her feet that friction, to protect her from blisters. On the trail in the wilderness, with no way to move but on your feet, a blister as small as a nickel could cripple and almost immobilize you.

Norman slowed for North Jenny Lake Junction and turned off. The one-way loop swung westward past String and Jenny lakes. The speed here dropped to only 25 mph. The bike lane was on the left. They were headed along narrowing sets of clearings, the trees moving in, until they merged into the dense forest that bracketed the lake. He reached under the front seat, trying to deflect only a splinter of his attention so that the road wasn't neglected for a moment. He pulled out a large heavyweight green garbage-pail liner and passed it back over the seat.

"This is for your stuff," Norman told them.

Ruth pulled it briskly out of his hand and dropped it on the floor on the pile of clothing. "I'm putting the bag on the floor, Norman," she said. "We'll have to leave it for last. If we don't have time you'll just have to do it. Like you said, it's more important we don't hold you up."

"Don't forget the dummies," he insisted. "I won't be able to do that."

"I'll do 'em now," she agreed. "Better get them out of the way." She accepted the two crumpled plastic bundles which grew under her breath into life-size inflatable dolls. They had found them advertised in a men's magazine as "companions." Ruth had to inflate them both because they gave Alice the shudders. When they were full she sat them in the front seat next to Norman, balanced wigs on the plastic heads, and draped some clothing over their shoulders and necks to give a vaguely dressed appearance.

They were getting warm, pulling on turtlenecks, wool shirts, grunting with exertion as they dressed in the narrow space. And finally covering everything with their parkas, because they didn't want to chance forgetting something in the rush of jumping out. They opened the rest of the windows to try to make it cooler.

The road forked as soon as they entered the woods. West was String Lake. Norman turned south. Trees on both sides now. The darkest stretch of road yet. "Just two minutes," he called out to them, like a conductor on a train. They were running a little late, but not badly. If everyone just kept moving it would be all right, he told himself.

"Money," Ruth announced. First she pulled the two partially loaded packs from the back and gave one to Alice. Then she unsnapped her floppy bag to expose the mound of bills.

"Guns," Alice corrected. "We said we'd put the guns on the bottom." Alice, looking battered but undaunted behind one shattered lens, unscrewed the barrel of the rifle and slid it into the waiting hole in the stock. Ruth started to disassemble her rifle too.

"I'm going to put the action in a side pocket," she said, unzipping a side section of her pack. "If I have to, I can use it like a pistol. I'd rather have that choice than not have it."

"I'd rather not have it," Alice said firmly. "If I took it I'd be sorry, so why bother to have it?"

"Why don't you throw it in the lake?" Norman asked. "Instead of having to carry it or having someone find it on you?"

"We can't." Alice made a wry face. "They're survival rifles. They're made to float." She stowed her gun as flatly as she could, leaning into the large, open cloth bag. She pulled out her pack stove and set it on the seat, so it wouldn't get buried underneath. And then she started to transfer the banded bills from her bag to the pack. Ruth did the same, stuffing handfuls of money as fast as she could. Norman slowed the car, starting to look for his marker. Sensing that they were almost done he wanted to give them more time. He didn't want to be parked for more than an instant. Stopping there could attract attention and might be remembered.

"This stuff weighs a ton," Alice complained. Her sense of weight was different from Ruth's. Alice was able to pick up an item and know whether, after hiking seven or eight miles and ascending several thousand feet, that item would still be treasured for its function or deeply resented for its weight.

"Do you have any more room? I'm getting full," Ruth said.

"I'm full too," Alice said seriously. "Don't load right to the top, either. All we need is for some of this to drop out." She patted the side pockets. They were full of small essentials they would need on the trail. They had condensed everything to the absolute minimum they considered safe, and they couldn't spare any of it just to generate a small amount of space. "Use the pockets of your parka," she advised. She opened her side pocket and discovered her gloves. She transferred them to an inside breast pocket and began to stuff bills into the outer ones. "Isn't this funny? We've stolen more money than we can carry out. Maybe we should go back and return the unused portion."

"Can we give it to Norman? No, Norman has to be clean," Ruth answered her own question. "Look, Norman, there's some money left here. We can't pack out every last drop. Can you get rid of it with the clothing? It's mostly singles anyway," she said scornfully.

Norman had spotted his mark, a segment of Mylar kite gleaming in a tree branch near the road. He had tied a short, heavy stick to the tail and heaved it up just the day before. The car was at a creep.

"Leave that and don't worry," he ordered them. "Look here. You have to get this right. That tree," and he pointed into the woods. They could see nothing. "It's right there, on the edge of the bank. The thickest trunk around. You'll see it when you get closer. It's right below there."

He stopped the car. The hum of the motor was the only sound in the woods for the moment. They all heard and understood that at the same instant. The women both moved at once, briskly and decisively. Quickly they rolled up their windows.

"Bless you, Norman," Alice called, squeezing him on the back of the neck as she shuffled across the car seat, pushing Ruth out before her with her knees, "See you tomorrow."

"Norman, you wait until we've found it," Ruth called back, worried.

"Shut that door! Be careful, don't let that dog out," he answered.

Ruth shouldered her pack through just one strap for the short walk to the edge of the lake. It was dark. Still no moonrise for more than half an hour, she figured, but it was possible to make her way through the trees for the thirty feet to the bank if she went slowly and concentrated very hard. She found a thick-bodied tree and held on to the trunk as she leaned over the bank and tried to see down the ten feet or so to the water. Nothing was there. She was sure she couldn't see a thing.

Norman was leaning across the seat, straining

his ears through the open window and toward the trees. "Okay." When he heard it, it was simple and distinct. No other sound. Had he heard rightly? He decided he had. He moved the car smoothly back onto the road and pulled the pad to him along the seat with one hand. "Fourteen minutes to Moose Gate," he read. He checked his watch. "It took a little over twenty-four minutes till now," he figured. Fourteen plus twenty-four was thirty-eight. Actually a little more. Subtract that from the guard's forty-five and it left seven minutes. Or actually a little less. That was his margin.

Ruth was standing at the bottom of the short steep bank trying to keep her hiking boots dry. They were triple waterproofed, repeatedly coated with wax and silicone paste and toasted over the kitchen stove to let it melt in. But immersing them in water before hiking in snow was still pushing it. There was no beach there, the hill dropped almost straight into the lake, but she dug her shoes into the earth slope and made herself a little step. Alice handed her pack down and Ruth dropped it into the tiny, black rubber raft that was tied there. Then she climbed into the front. Alice took her place on the ledge, but when Ruth reached out a hand to help her into the boat, Alice refused it. Instead she put her head back and breathed deeply, once, and again, and with her eyes closed this time, once again.

"Hurry up," Ruth called a bit snappishly, but Alice paid no attention. She rocked her hips side to side, settling her weight, feeling the cleats on her shoes working into the soft earth, anchoring her. Just from the feel she could tell there was a soft evergreen mulch under her, organic matter slowly breaking down into sweet, rich earth. Ruth waited, not really understanding until she saw Alice's body ripple like a horse's flank in a long shudder. And only then did Alice open her eyes.

"I feel so much better out here," she said with relief. "You have no idea." And in truth, her face did look much more alive and real than it had. This time she did take Ruth's hand and stepped out. There was the inevitable moment of sliding and sharp rocking as she tried to find her balance among all the objects around her feet. But when she sat down, wedging her behind into a rounded corner and shifting her pack to lie half over her leg, the raft suddenly felt not only quite stable but also beautifully comfortable. A little water bed in the wilderness.

She switched on the electric trolling motor. The hum was almost lost in the light breeze. The vibration of the engine and the motion soothed all the knots which the last hours had tied. They shifted about a bit more, working their legs onto the edge of the raft to rest them and spread out more comfortably. They didn't speak. Occasionally it felt good to sigh. The fifteen-minute trip across Jenny Lake was saving them over two hours hiking around it in the night. And all on schedule. They were covered in their crossing by the dark of the moonless night. The moon wouldn't rise for more than half an hour yet, not until they would need it. They were heading almost due west, to just below Inspiration Point, a wooded protrusion at the mouth of Cascade Canyon. Their eyes were adjusting now and even by starlight it would be easy to find. And they they should still have some good dark minutes left to complete preparations and set out before moonrise. But in the meantime there was nothing to do but relax, to let the mind float as freely as the body. And they glided through the night, stately and still, like two queens on a barge drifting down some ancient river.

Sunday 9:16 P.M.

The clothing and the wigs. His own drag outfit! The dog! The money! The crap in the car was many times over what was needed to incriminate him. The only answer was to make sure he got it all, and himself, out the gate before they sealed it and began the search. All he could do now was complete his part and hope everything went well. He drove at the limit, one eye on the speedometer and one on his watch, trying constantly to estimate if he was ahead or behind.

There were only a few little things he could do to speed it along. One at a time he brought his feet up to where he could reach them and undid his pumps. He dropped them in the back with the women's clothing so it would be all in one place. It took him the rest of the way to the gate to remove his panty hose without slacking off on the gas pedal. He braked awkwardly for the gate, and the dummies which had been swaying so agreeably on the seat next to him suddenly fell forward and bounced headfirst into the dash. He swept them up with a backhand, settling them again with his arm. Their wigs were crooked but they would have to do. It was still dark and the light from the little booth caught only the driver's face.

"Stop and Proceed," the sign said. There was only one ranger, cute little hat serious across his forehead like bangs, in the far booth. He was selling passes to incoming cars. All was peaceful. Norman rolled to a stop halfway into the lane, hesitated, forcing his foot to hold the brake for the instant and touching the horn lightly. The ranger looked up and Norman wiggled his fingers in a flirty too-dle-oo and smiled at him. Three little maids, all in a row, one with cockleshells. And a lanky Lauren Bacall of a dog. "Remember us, darling," he promised under his breath, "and we'll not forget thee." And then he passed through, into freedom, and into the welcoming dark. About fifteen more minutes until moonrise, he figured.

The ranger center, the park headquarters, was just ahead on the left, maybe an eighth of a mile down the road. He took that turn off the main way. No one was out. He went past the main building and its parking lot, now striped with ranger wagons, and on down to the raft landing area. A few dark vehicles were clumped at the other end, near the ramp. The van was on the close side, just where they had left it earlier. He pulled right alongside of it.

Now he had to be organized. There was too much to do to remember it all. Or to think about it as he went along. Drill would save him now. And he had been so lazy and halfhearted when they were rehearsing drill. He had been so sure he had it all under control. He cursed himself for smugness, for laxness, for being undisciplined and self-indulgent. "If they catch me I'll never tell who I was with," he promised himself in atonement, imagining himself dying nobly, tortured to death by the police, and immediately realized how easy it would be to trace any one of them to the rest.

Dog first, he decided, and hopefully everything else would follow automatically after. "Here, boy," he called several times softly over the back of the front seat, making assorted motions with his hands to signal the dog to jump up forward. The waving and gesturing which was so irritatingly self-evident to him meant nothing to the dog, however. It was symbolic communication, he realized. A form of language. Like when he would sometimes point at a stick he wanted a dog to fetch, and the dog would look only at the end of his waving finger. Now the dog was confused, but good-natured, and willing to play. It sat back on its haunches and set its long front legs stiffly out, ready to scamper wildly to the right or left, chase or be chased, depending on how the game developed. This isn't going to work, Norman realized, and gave in, climbing gracelessly into the back seat with his long dress binding his ankles.

The dog rolled its eyes at being cornered and looked for an open corridor. But Norman didn't give it time to escalate the chaos and grabbed the leash firmly and pulled the dog forward with a no-nonsense, we'll-talk-about-this-later-but-you'll-do-what-I-want-now attitude beamed directly at the animal. It understood completely and complied.

Norman got out, scurried quickly to the van, keeping his head low as if that would help him now, and half guided, half lifted the dog through the side door. He broke open one of the cellophane bags of dog food he had been using and dropped it in a pile on the floor. The dog began to wolf it down immediately. "Eat and be quiet," Norman

told him. "You'll get your water in a little while,"
he promised.

He shut the van door and leaped back into the
wagon, hopping awkwardly since the pebbles were
digging into his bare feet. Into the rear seat now,
because the door was open, and because there
would probably be more room, although he was
supposed to be in the front. It probably wouldn't
make any difference, but he had no time to think
about it. He wanted to be done before the moon
came up, and this was only the beginning.

The dress came over his head and the wig with
it in a single motion that pleased him. Not so
pleasing were the welts the tape left on his chest,
and the short violent struggle with his girdle. His
clothing was in a paper bag on the transmission
hump in front and he pulled it back to him. Pen-
dleton, dungarees, hiking shoes, mustache, he put
them on as rapidly as he could, always checking
ahead to the next item before he was ready for it
so his hands wouldn't be idle for an instant. No
devil's playthings his. His mother would be proud.

He started to reach forward again and then remembered it was already back there. On the floor,
Ruth had said. He groped around under his dress
until he found the plastic garbage bag. Everything
went in, bundled and clumped, hoping that it
would be such a mess as to be unrecognizable if
someone did ever look. The women's bags with the
remainder of the money were near the bottom, he
made sure. And then his drag and their drag and
the dummies, deflated and wadded together. The
large jar of cold cream they had left on the seat.
He pulled the foam dice from where they hung
on the rearview mirror and then, checking the area

for activity again and trusting, more than actually seeing, that all was well, he got out and dropped the bag on the ground next to the car.

Really putting his back into it now he walked around the car stripping the wood-grained contact paper from the sides and leaving the basic sage green finish underneath. The foxtail, no longer pink in the dark, caught his eye and he tore it off and stuffed it in the sack with the rest. He went to the van and got a quart jar of mustard. The dog looked up, curious, but it was becoming accustomed to the frantic activity which had constantly surrounded it for the last hours. It sat, alert but still, apparently willing to wait for things to settle into firmer places before it made any moves.

Norman opened the mustard jar and emptied it into the sack, throwing the container in after it. He mushed everything around so the mustard was more or less spread, tied a double knot in the top of the bag, and carried it to one of the trash containers by the side of the lot.

"Almost done, now," he reassured himself as he trotted back to the wagon. "Almost . . ." The National Park Service emblem he had so painstakingly copied onto contact paper came from his little stash in the front, along with several other items he piled on the seat to be ready. The emblems were pretty good, he felt, but no one really looked at them anyway. That was the nature of official materials of any kind. But they did have to be on straight. That would matter. He forced himself to slow down while he carefully spread them on both sides of the automobile. "Not bad. They'll do," he comforted himself. The closer he got to finishing, the later it got also. And the tenser. He was having awful visions of a photo finish. Like having a tie in a race with an express train.

The license plates came off the seat next. The little double-stick fastening pads were firmly behind the plates, ready to be peeled and slapped over the plates on the stolen vehicle. These were the government plates from the park vehicles, at home in the woods and even, perhaps, this very lot.

And then the last item. The plastic bubble and heavy chrome base of the red-top was the only thing left. He remembered when he had bought that red-top in an auto-wrecking yard in Oakland. He had unscrewed it from the roof of an old security patrol car. "Damn!" They had forgotten to put the stick-'em pads on the bottom and he didn't know where they were now. And he wasn't inclined to waste time looking. He set it on the roof, centering it with the scratch marks he had made for just that purpose, and jumped into the car with the feeling of leaping out of a second-story window and onto the back of a horse.

The sound was sickening. As he shot away, as he began to move at all, as a matter of fact, he was already telling his foot to hit the brake and stop. The rumble of the red-top as it tumbled across the roof wasn't nearly as bad as waiting for it to hit the ground as it landed. God damn! he thought, in agony. This could blow it. He didn't even want to think about it just then, the implications seemed so paralyzing to him. It could screw up everything. He couldn't tell from the sound, but he was outside and checking before it had completely stopped rolling. The red plastic top was uncrushed. That was all that mattered. Two novenas, he promised. He put it next to him and drove back, across the adjoining parking lot, and right to ranger headquarters. There was a row of similar light green wagons there, as well as others scattered, but he headed for that group. It was the most concentrated. And it was the most sheltering. The floodlights that covered the lot were masked by the corner of the building and these cars were in shadow, less distinct than the others for the remainder of the night.

He passed through a bright band of direct light on his way to the dark, caught a glance of his eye, ear, and forehead in the rearview mirror, and almost turned in horror to see who was sitting behind him. But it was himself, the heavily mascaraed eye, the pancake makeup, the carmine lips an ugly black in the artificial light, the rich rhinestone pendant earrings. And just the end of a rough, masculine mustache.

He swung in an arc, tires almost squealing, to back into a space to match the other cars. A side door of the station bounced open and voices came clearly across the night air. They hadn't heard him because they were so excited with the robbery alert. This had to work, he realized, or it would all end right here.

He cut the engine immediately. The red-top was next. He lifted it out of the window and onto the roof, somewhere, and dropped it almost immediately. No time for niceties now. It was on the roof.

Then the windows. He rolled his side first, locking all doors. Then he threw himself across the front seat, hitting the buttons and rolling up the other window, keeping his head as low as the voices came nearer, nearer than touching, it seemed, nearer than tolerable, waiting still like a hare in panic, trying not to bolt. And then he rolled off, just as he saw shoulders and corners of heads, rolled into the narrow space in front of the front seat, pedals digging into his leg, face down, pulling off his reflective earrings and lying still with his breathing and praying the dog back at the van didn't bark. He never wanted to see the look Alice would give him if that dog blew it.

A hand came out of the dark and seized his door handle.

"Over here," someone corrected, drawing the uniformed arm over to another wagon.

"Whose is this?" the puzzled voice demanded.

"I don't know. Come on," was the merciful reply. It had only taken an instant, but even an instant is enough when balanced on a razor blade.

Engines began to cough and kick over, like heavy smokers waking, and then without warm-up, wagons roared away. The voices and engines mixed, and then just the engines, and then nothing. He remembered the stories where someone's hair turned gray in an instant. He didn't believe them. But he would remember to glance in the mirror anyway. There was sand and dirt stuck to his right cheek where he had ground it into the floor, seeking an extra quarter inch of distance. He raised his head a bit and brushed it off as best he could.

He took a cautious look around. He definitely didn't want to show this face there if he could help it. It had been so close. He couldn't help but wonder, despite his godlessness and blasphemy, if he wasn't under some special protection, reserved perhaps for some great purpose.

Most of the wagons were gone now. No one was about at that moment and he couldn't afford to wait any longer. As he got out he straightened the red-top, locked the door, and took off at a lope. He ran bent over, as if ducking bullets. And then down the short stretch of road to the van, now splendidly alone, innocent-looking, familiar, and non-criminal in the night.

"Shit, I threw away the cold cream," he remembered, sorting through his options for a makeup remover. There was suntan lotion in the glove compartment, he remembered. And Crisco in the van. The widemouthed can with its generous handfuls of lubrication seemed especially sweet to him at that moment. He smeared it across his face and scraped vigorously at his skin with the towel.

As he put the towel down he finally felt himself relax a bit. The worst was over now. The dog. He still had to get rid of the dog. Just the same he sat there for a minute after he had checked his face carefully in the mirror again. Basically he was all right now. Almost, but compared to before, basically. He put his mustache back on slowly and carefully, trying to feel what his muscles and organs were doing, daring for the first time to ask, letting them release their complaints into his consciousness, soothing them, and reassuring them that it was mostly over.

Then he started his engine and drove slowly out, down the lane, past the ranger headquarters, and onto the road back to town. Looking back he could just make out the forms of rangers pulling the black-and-white-striped sawhorse barricades out to block the tollbooths. Cars would be coming through one at a time now, just to be double sure, each checked out carefully in a show of official zeal. It was a double check, just to be extra careful, but it was mostly for show just the same. The guard at the gate had seen them leave, all three. Whoever and whatever they were.

Keeping an eye on the rearview mirror he had to pull off twice as ranger wagons barreled down the road past him, sirens and red-tops making their harsh announcements to the mountain night. "Go get 'em!" he cheered them on, giving them room for their speed.

When the road looked clear, both ahead and behind, he found a scenic turnoff and pulled in. He was kind of sad to see the dog go, but keeping him was out of the question. The animal followed obediently as he drew it by the leash. "Now you have lots of room for a good run. There's water out there. And if you're sharp, maybe you can snag a rabbit. Imagine telling everybody in Idaho Falls about *that*." He looked for a stick to throw but couldn't see anything which would serve. He finally settled for a rock. He climbed back into the van immediately, not waiting to see the animal streaking into the dark.

Norman remembered the last entry on the yellow pad, now crumpled and coated with mustard in the trash bin: "Moose to Jackson, 15 min. at 50 mph." Straight on down the John D. Rockefeller Parkway.

Jackson would be hopping, crowded, and confused on this last weekend of the season. Usually bars closed at 10:00 P.M. on Sunday, but this was one of the four weekends they stayed open until 2:00 A.M. His stomach would be in shape for a drink by the time he got there. And then on to wait at the Teton campground on the other side of the range, near the Idaho border.

Sunday 9:28 P.M.

The crossing had been more than easy, it had been
quite pleasant. Alice tensed a bit as she guided the
boat to the point of land, a small delta for Cascade
Creek where it emptied its glacial water into the
lake. This was one of the most popular hiking
areas in the park. An easy walk around the lake. It
wasn't too late for someone to be wandering
about. But there was no one there. A loaf of rock
jutting into the lake let them land without risking
the raft bottom in shallow water. Ruth climbed out
first and took the packs as they were handed to her.
Neither of them spoke. It was safer, but even given
that, neither of them wanted to break the peace
they had finally found.

Squatting by the water, Alice passed the fat
rim of the raft from hand to hand until it was
turned around and pointing back toward the other
shore. They had forgotten completely about the
paddles, which had a slight positive flotation so
they wouldn't sink if dropped. Well, they would
look even stranger if they were found with the
paddles up in the canyon, she decided. Better leave
them here and trust to luck. Even if they did float
back up, the presence of a paddle or two in the
lake wouldn't seem particularly suspicious. The

handles were secured through the rowing loops so she pulled the blades into the boat and wedged them there. The automobile battery which powered the motor would drag the whole mess to the bottom and hold it down. Or so she hoped. She pulled the plugs on all chambers, started the motor, and pointed the boat across the lake. They waited, watching it sail smoothly on, out of reach now, beginning to wonder if it might not cross the lake again and lie on the opposite shore to tell their secret. But just on the edge of vision it ceased to make progress, wallowing with a slightly different tone, receding no more, but settling instead. And then gone.

"Well, here we are," Ruth finally said. Her voice was low, but like her eyes, it was dancing, even taking little hops. She was excited by their success.

"Uh-huh!" Alice grinned back at her. It felt great to be outside and to have it all over. She hadn't felt this alive in weeks.

"You realize, of course, that you just sank more than five hundred dollars' worth of equipment out there."

"We can afford it," Alice consoled her. "We probably have over a hundred thousand in our packs." More grinning. Eyes dancing with eyes.

Ruth peered into the night woods, the trail not at all inviting to her city vision. "Just where did you say that helicopter was going to pick us up?"

"Ho ho," Alice mocked. "Just find a phone booth and call a cab." She checked her watch and led them off slowly. No sign yet. It was difficult to tell exactly when because it depended on just where the moon would clear the mountains around them. They set off up the trail, into the trees immediately, groping their way because the foliage cut off even the starlight. They wanted to climb well away from the shore by the time the moon lighted the trail. Then they could start to hike in earnest. The further they went the less likelihood they would meet anyone, or the less it would be likely to matter.

Alice felt an excitement in her body as she began to move. This was where she felt right. She looked forward to building up a light sweat, stuffing her parka under some pack strap to hang out of her way, and simplifying her attention to only striding and breathing. That was the best. And all the rest was a poor second to that aliveness. This has to be one of the healthiest robberies in history, she thought.

Sunday 9:50 P.M.

Bill Shaw was a big man, and that made his job easier. He had a thick neck, and the heavy silver watchband inlaid with turquoise pointed out how thick his wrists were too. He always carried an expensive pair of Ray-Bans in their case. All his equipment was good, he always took good care of it, and he did a good job. People in the park and the larger community respected the head ranger. When his name came up someone inevitably talked of how sharp he was as a cop, and how intelligent. He never did anything to discourage this.

Bill Shaw saw his territory as a special situation. There were high walls of mountain all along the east and west. The opening at the north led direct-ly into Yellowstone, another national park. To the east was Targhee Pass. And to the south there were only two basic routes away. The Wilson Road was thin and winding, suitable in its better parts only for drunks in sports cars, and in its worst stretches barely passable. (It ran in front of the Rockefeller JY Ranch, and it was a local rumor that to insure their privacy they had blocked en-tirely the paving of several miles of rough dirt near the midpoint.) The other road ran exposed through the elk refuge, and into Jackson. The area beyond was also mountainous. The valley was a sealed box with slow leaks at either end.

Since escape was not one of the practical alternatives of the area, there was almost no premeditated crime, and even the impulsive crimes tended to be light and casual. In that environment the criminal and the investigator were locked together. New employees were almost always the culprits and they had to work on, straight-faced and pretending calm, while they watched Bill Shaw around them. And he always went seriously, determinedly, and methodically about his job, in full view where everyone could watch.

It was not from vanity. Most of his vanities were pleasures he took privately, like being able to hold his liquor, being a tender lover, and having a knowing hand with horses. But he used his public presence as a tool. He did not think he was as intelligent as they said. So he let his reputation radiate like electricity around him, waiting for that additional factor that multiplied his efforts, when the "criminal" saw him and was impressed, and either confessed or did something to give himself away in that pressure-cooked situation.

"Hi, Bill."

"Hello, Bill."

The two rangers spotted him before he crossed more than a few feet into the lobby. He was certain they had been keeping an eye on the door just to impress him. They wanted to be noticed. And it was their way of letting him know they were alert. They were both in their mid-twenties, career men, still simple and earnest in their approach, and totally unaware of it. Well, Chuck was. Ryner was a bit older. He already had been around awhile.

Everyone just called him Ryner, of course. Certain people didn't seem like first-name types, for some reason. They called him "Ryner" to his face, but some called him "The Shadow" behind his back. They always had a few like him, people who didn't mix well, who preferred night work, who tended to prowl around in the evenings even when they were off duty. Because of that Bill didn't see him much. He should really get to know the man better. But he had to deal with ninety rangers and had a force of over three hundred in the field.

Still he was glad to see that they had been assigned to work together this night. Probably some supervisor following his lead, for almost instinctively he paired them as often as possible. Chuck really was one of the kids, essentially sweet-natured, if sometimes a bit slow. He bumbled things with predictable regularity, but people liked him and forgave him, and he deserved that consideration because he really meant well.

Ryner was unquestionably brighter. But he could be gruff and abrasive. Just the opposite of Chuck, he could do the best thing in the worst way and get the wrong results. Between the two of them, when they were working in harmony, they created a single, excellent ranger, and he was quite satisfied with that, felt that was as much as you had any right to expect, human nature being what it was.

And then too there was the elk business. No one had told him, although the whole staff was passing it on at one point. He had overheard it, sitting at his desk. He even had a sense that it was something he was meant to overhear. That the staff wanted him to know, but no one wanted to come directly and tell him. He didn't know if the story was true or not. And he didn't want to let gossip warp his dealings with anyone. So he put the matter out of his mind.

He watched as Chuck left the line of guests he had been questioning and came quickly over to him. Ryner was standing by the accounting-office door as if he were guarding it. Big, with a thick, hard body, hypertensive red face, brown brush cut, he somehow made his ranger attire look more like a state police uniform.

"I thought we should get right on it," Chuck said. In his eagerness he reminded Bill of a puppy that might wet on itself.

"I've covered almost everyone," Chuck went on, "and I have a list of those who think they saw something. Should I send the others back to their rooms, do you think?"

"Thank them for their cooperation. And we don't need to send them to their rooms. These people are here on their vacations. Take their statements and ID's. Then come and tell me what you've got. Where's Diane and the accountant?"

He walked the length of the lobby to the office Chuck pointed out for him. He was left-handed and wearing his gun in a holster on his left hip. One of the employees noticed it and mentioned it to someone else: you could count on the fingers of one hand the number of times he had worn that gun in the last seven or eight years. It was pretty much quiet until he went into the doorway under the stairs. Employees and guests alike were properly respectful, enjoying a good robbery. He looked up and nodded briefly to Ryner as he went in.

Diane and Mike were in the larger office, just inside the door. There was more air than in the smaller one by the safe. And they wanted that room left undisturbed. The accountant sat in a swivel chair and a doctor, one of the convention guests actually, had pulled another chair up to it and was applying a small bandage, using a first-aid kit someone had found in an office nearby.

Bill nodded at the two rangers and went up to the accountant. "I heard you got hit. How is it? Will we be able to talk tonight?" he asked politely.

Allen nodded. "It wasn't a bad knock," the doctor explained for him. "He should be all right. Better get it X-rayed tomorrow just to be safe though." The doctor naturally assumed his authority over the patient and felt equal to the police. It looked a little incongruous though, since he was dressed for the convention and worked over Allen awkwardly, holding his body fastidiously back to make sure he didn't dirty his clothing. He was wearing freshly pressed burgundy pants with a white vinyl belt, white shoes with a small gold clasp for decoration, a peach shirt with a dark blue tie, and the matching blue jacket was draped carefully over the back of his chair. Double-knit from his toes to his nose.

Bill walked back to Diane while the doctor was finishing up. "What's going on, Diane?"

"I think the doorman has more to say. There was an outrageous scene in the lobby while this was going on. Probably a diversion. Might have been a guy dressed up like a woman." Bill shook his head incredulously. "The doorman saw two

women get into a car he was driving and they all
left together. This fellow here doesn't have much
except a partial description of the women, and
that seems to change a little each time he goes
over it, so I don't know. And he feels they were
pretty nice to him."

"After they smashed him like that?"

"That's what he feels."

"No accounting for taste." Bill shrugged, looking
disgusted that there were apparently some men
who liked being hit by women. Personally, he
couldn't see it. "What's his name again?"

"Allen something. Oh, he thought one woman
called the other one Norman," she added.

Bill looked at her with irritation, then sighed
and gathered his energy for a long sustained push.
He had just settled down to an evening of beer
and television and it took a major effort to change
direction so drastically. But the only way to do it
was to do it. "Diane, would you run up to the
kitchen and get us a big pot of coffee and a tray
of cups? I think we're going to be here for a
while."

"What should I do?" Mike asked brightly, after
she had left.

Bill looked at him, a bit amazed that the summer worker didn't have sense enough to walk away
and disappear. "Why don't you help your aunt,"
he said after a minute.

"Get in touch with personnel," Bill was saying
when they came back with their load. Bill had gotten rid of the accountant quickly, because something about the man, he didn't know what, made
him nervous. The doorman had been easier. And
now he was sending out the eager ranger and his

serious partner again. "We want the file Polaroids
on everyone who has worked here. Go back five
years. Or seven. Use your judgment when you see
how many there are. Remember, you'll have to
show them all to everyone. And many of the ap-
plicants who weren't hired attached photos to their
applications. They don't have to but many do anyway. Get those, too." He sighed again. "Might as
well bring all the photos, men and women. Some
of the people think one of them was really a man."
The thought made him tired for some reason.
"Show 'em to Allen and the doorman first, and
then let the guests play with them. I'll be here for
a while and then I'm going back to headquarters.
Be sure to find me when you're done."

"Thanks," he said to Diane and Mike, taking his
first cup of hot coffee and going to the phone with
it. "Hi, Artie," he said to the sheriff a few seconds
later. "This is Bill Shaw. Have you heard what's
been going on up here?" He waited a minute and
smiled automatically at the inevitable wisecracks,
even though the sheriff couldn't see his face with
its polite, good-natured gesturing. "Well, we've
blocked our gates, but it's mostly for the newspapers, so we can tell them when they ask what
we're doing. Our man on Moose said he saw them
go through. Green, wood-paneled wagon, Dodge,
late model. Foxtail. We got the APB right out.
Three women, dressed to the hilt. One of them may
be—" He was interrupted by a squawking which
came with irritating harshness from the earpiece.
"You heard about that, eh?" he said, squinting
until the unpleasant sound stopped. "Yes. Yes. No,
we don't know for sure yet, one way or the other.
Yes, it looks like it was an inside thing, or con-

nected in some way. They always are up here, don't you know. Say, how would you like to come and work along together on this? We could stay tighter if we could coordinate better." He waited a second. "Why don't we meet at Moose headquarters then? Thanks, Artie. I'll be along in a little while. Have to notify the FBI man. . . . Yes . . . Well, that's how it is with us poor naïve little rangers. Just country, don't you know. I'll see you in about an hour then. . . . Yes, this is a bit of a weird one all right. Amateurs, no question. No one else would try such a weird stunt and all. . . . Well, I'll see you then. Bye."

He grimaced to himself after he put the phone down. Diane and Mike were still there when he looked up. "Thanks for the coffee," he said again automatically. "You two can knock off now. Don't you have anything to get ready for tomorrow?"

"No, I'm off," Diane replied. "Listen, Bill, we saw as much as anyone."

"What did *you* see?"

"Well, right after my lecture we were coming through the lobby and we passed two women who were all made up and talking, and we didn't think a lot about it at the time because this person came in with the dog just then, but afterward I—"

"This person. This person!" Bill interrupted her in exasperation. "What do you mean by 'this person'?"

"The person who was all dressed up in the gown with the Afghan . . ." she answered defensively, a bit cowed by his vehemence.

"My God! A whole lobby full of doctors and their wives, any one of whom should be able to pass a sex-identification test blindfolded, and they can't agree on whether 'this person' was a man or a woman. Can you believe it? What's so hard, for Christ's sake"—he would regret that; he never cursed on the job—"about telling the difference between a man and a woman? Has the world changed so much in the past few years that a little thing like that is no longer common knowledge? One doctor even had the nerve to tell me he thought it was a woman made up to look like a man impersonating a woman. Where are we going to get with thinking like that? Was it a man or a woman? You're a woman. You should know one if you see one, shouldn't you?"

"I don't know." She brushed the question aside. "Listen, Bill, I'm trying to tell you something. I overheard one of those women—or at least I think it was one of those women and I could cross-check it with Allen to make sure—I heard one of them say, well, one of them stumbled in her high shoes and the other said, 'You'd better remember to always keep two points,' or something like that. Two points, Bill, like ice-ax talk, glacier-crossing, snow-climbing talk. That's not a city joke. She was a technical climber. She had to be. In spite of those clothes. It's the only thing that makes sense of it all. I've been thinking about it and that pulls it all together. And then I looked back at them as they passed." She was getting breathless now, winded from talking uphill against his skepticism and from trying so hard to change the look on his face, the kindly, patient, fatherly, tolerant, exasperated, superior look that said his mind was already elsewhere, on his work, and waiting politely for her to finish. "I looked back and I saw this mark on her back." She had slowed now, realizing she was burning herself out, knowing from experience that she had to slack off, that there was no point in banging her head against walls. "It was a rope burn, right across her back, as if she had been rappelling this summer. She's a technical climber, I think, Bill. Do you see what I mean?"

He looked at her seriously and for an instant she thought he was thinking about what she had said. "You have a master's in biology and you can't even tell me if it was a man or woman," he finally said tiredly and with a touch of self-pity. "And now you want to tell me that two bubbleheads who breeze in here and pop our little resort are not what they seem either. Maybe they were all marionettes which were controlled by the dog: a ventriloquist who was really two midgets under a fur blanket. Oh, this will be a long night. I just know this will be one of those long nights." He shrugged and turned away from them.

Then he turned back, his face genuinely concerned now. "Why don't you go home and get a good night's sleep, Diane? And take your nephew with you. I'm sorry I was cross with you. I really am. It's the pressure and the fact I'm going to have to work right through the night on this one. And I was all set to take it easy tonight. You're one of my best little workers." He gave her a secret wink. "You know that, don't you?" He put his arm around her shoulders and gave a squeeze. "This will all be over before sunrise. These weirdos have no chance out here in our country and before tomorrow they'll be sorry they ever came here. So why don't you forget all about this and enjoy your day off? Are you going hiking tomorrow?"

"Perhaps," she answered stiffly. Even though she

almost always did. It was one of the things that made the job worthwhile. And he had even clicked off an idea in her head when he said that. She made no movement of acquiescence but just stood there patiently until her boss let go of her, shrugged, and went out the door.

"You stay at my place tonight," she told Mike without explanation. "I want to get an early start tomorrow."

"Don't you want to stick around and see what happens?"

"You heard the man. You won't miss anything. It will all be over before you open your sleepy eyes in the morning. And this will be your last weekend here this season. Let's not waste it following Captain Shaw around."

Sunday 9:53 P.M.

They had become moles, burrowing through the night. Or so it seemed to Alice as she followed Ruth. She had sent Ruth ahead so she could keep an eye on her. Ruth had said she was just fine, but from the rear the tall figure revealed with her posture and rhythm what she had denied with her voice. She was bent almost over, much more than the gentle slope demanded, balancing the pack on the curving, almost horizontal shelf of her back, rather than carrying it. "She needs to adjust that," Alice thought, concerned that Ruth didn't realize the fact herself, feel it clearly in her own body. "That will tire her out in no time, hauling it like that."

It wouldn't hurt to go on that way for a little while, she decided. Better to leave her alone for a bit than to fuss over her too much. Woods and mountains were new enough for Ruth. She could easily be made to feel incompetent, helpless. Frightened. Discouraged. The list could go on, depending on how tough things got. A little further up, when they stopped for a short rest, was the natural time to adjust packs and boots, to tighten up where there was shifting and rubbing, to loosen where there was cutting, binding, interrupted circulation. And maybe Ruth would take care of it herself then. That would be better. She probably realized it, Alice comforted herself, and didn't want to stop yet, didn't want to lose that time right at the start.

Still, she continued to watch Ruth with concern, calculating the adjustments which would make her more comfortable. It was only comfort at first. After a bit, the chafing, the energy lost in poor balance and pain, all could make little complaints much more serious. And there was no getting off the trail and into a comfortable chair, a warm bed, a hot bath. They had to live with anything that developed, and continue in spite of it.

"The belly band," she decided. She needed to loosen the shoulder straps and tighten the belly band. The wide, thickly padded belt that was now a part of any good pack was designed to place 80 to 90 percent of the pack weight on the hips. It should be cinched up as tightly as a saddle, placing the weight solidly onto those thick thigh muscles which were so well suited to bearing the load. Ruth, on the other hand, like many novices, looked at a pack and thought "logically" that the weight should be carried high, several feet up her long, thin back, supported on the narrow ridges of her shoulders. But the shoulder straps should only be tight enough to balance the pack and keep it riding close to her body. The weight should be on her hips. That's why she was having trouble now. She knew better, if she would think. Or rather, feel. They had been over this, practiced it in the lower, more accessible slopes of the Sierra Nevada, but she had forgotten apparently. It was probably the excitement.

And so they had become moles. Ruth trying unsuccessfully to tunnel out from under the cloth and aluminum mound that almost covered her, pressing her down, and Alice, who followed right behind, flicking her eyes from Ruth to the trail under her feet and back to Ruth.

It was the strain of the whole weekend, because it certainly wasn't the trail. The path went along Cascade Creek and was so well trampled that, moving cautiously, they were still able to follow it in the dark. Everyone came here, it seemed, during the season. At least everyone willing to go to the trouble of getting out of his recreation vehicle. The second bridge left them just below Hidden Falls. They could hear it clearly above the creek's sound. There were smaller, unmarked trails leading off to the left for viewing the falls. They had come half a mile already, the little meter in her head ticked off.

That led right into the switchbacks up to Inspiration Point. The switchbacks, or zigzags, were the climbers' way of reducing a steep slope to more reasonable proportions, taking it in short traverses, back and forth, rather than trying to scramble straight up. The latter method would soon wear down a slippery chute, dangerous to ascend or descend, and readily eroded to a gulley by spring rains. At the climb Ruth just plowed determinedly ahead without pausing for rest, and again Alice had not wanted to interrupt her. Now it was steep. But it was only another half-mile to the top, and then they would have more than three miles through the canyon along the creek side, an easy and almost level walk. That should give her a rest.

They had been climbing steadily, preoccupied

with effort, when Alice realized that the trail was
suddenly emerging clearly before her. The moon
was finally coming out! She stopped and raised
her head with a sense of profound relief. She suddenly felt out from under. They were just cresting
the glacial bench that was Inspiration Point, a
steep cliff overlooking the valley. She had been
there in the daytime before, but never at night.
And she scolded herself for burying her head in
worries when she was in the mountains. That was
a form of irreverence to her, close to what she
meant by "sacrilege."

She stopped, as the trail leveled off, and turned
back, first just her head, and then her entire body.
There was a slight haze over the Hole, wispy, not
solid. Just a night mist, she figured. The moon
was softened as it emerged, huge and radiant, but
its strange, almost green-gray light coated everything she could see: the magic valley they had
left. the magic mountains they were entering.

This was a glacial canyon they were climbing;
the fluting and hollows which had been scraped
and smoothed by aeons of prehistoric ice were now
again polished by the spreading icy light. From this
height Jenny Lake, almost directly below them,
revealed its glacial history. The ridge on the far
side, the glacial moraine of earth and gravel and
rock which had been pushed up and left there by
the melting ice to form the natural dam which
created the lake, was clearly visible. That was also
the source of soil for the dense ring of conifers
that banded the water. Melting glacier and snow
water still filled the depression.

But it was upward that she strained to see,
bending her head back until it pressed against the

pack frame, and then leaning her whole body back
further to see still higher. The floor of the canyon
sloped up from behind the stream at almost forty-
five degrees for several hundred yards. And then
the mountains themselves began, enormous rocks,
continuous for a mile above her head. Teewinot,
the Grand, and Mount Owen, seeming the most
solid and ancient things she had ever seen. Cosmic,
she thought. Cosmic, like the stars, only right here.
And we're climbing into their laps, onto their
shoulders, like children. All she and Ruth and Norman had done and planned and worried about
suddenly seemed so blissfully trivial.

She remembered Ruth, and with her emotions
already opened by what she saw around her she
felt a sad and sympathetic wrench for her friend.
Ruth had not even noticed the break in the foot-
steps behind her. Steadily, determinedly, she had
plugged on, looking joyless and exerting great effort. "Not everyone feels reborn here," Alice reminded herself. "Not everyone sees it the way I
do." She jogged along at double speed and it didn't
take her long to overtake her trudging companion.
She took hold of her shoulder. It would have been
easier to grab her pack, in fact it was difficult to
reach around the great bulge on her back, but she
wanted to touch her arm. Ruth just stopped, head
still down, catching her breath, and Alice waited
a moment before she turned her around gently.
She gestured upward. "Ruth, the moon is coming
up."

Ruth took a single look and then nodded.

"Are you all right?"

Ruth nodded again but her eyes looked pained.
She was concentrating on catching her breath.

"Let's take a break," Alice said. She checked around them. They could stop right there. No one else should be out. And they couldn't climb off the trail at night. She unbuckled her belly band, feeling a familiar ache where the flesh had been compressed at her hips. And then she wriggled free of the shoulder straps, lowered her pack to the ground, and went to help her friend. It would have been easier to rest with the packs on, and faster, but she didn't want to take the chance that Ruth would go on with her pack as before. And this would give them a better rest. Alice felt fresh, as if she were just beginning to warm up, but Ruth looked as if she could use a real stop.

She helped Ruth slide her pack off, sparing her the weight and effort of lowering it to the ground. She leaned it against a rock with the cloth side out and patted it with her hands like a pillow, directing her friend. Obediently, Ruth sat down next to it and leaned back on the cushioning and insulating pack body. It was the closest they would come to a comfortable chair until they were out of the mountains. Ruth's breathing, while no longer labored, still seemed uneven and unsatisfying.

"How's your period?"

"Oh," she seemed to remember, "not too bad. I have some cramps."

"You don't look too good."

"I'll be all right."

"Nobody needs a martyr. What feels wrong?" She looked at Ruth, who seemed to be deciding what to say. "I need to know how you feel. I don't want to play games," she said seriously.

"Everything's a little wrong. My stomach, my head. My legs and my lungs. Everything. But nothing really bad. I just have to get loosened up. I haven't got my rhythm yet."

"Does resting help?"

She thought a minute. "Not really. I feel like I'd just like to get it over as soon as possible. Then I'll feel better." She looked at Alice and laughed apologetically. "Too much excitement for me."

"I know. Deep down you're just sweet and helpless. Well, let's stay here for another few minutes anyway. I could use the stop even if you can't. The next three and a half miles are really easy. We have plenty of light and we can take it slow. It'll be okay."

Ruth leaned back and shut her eyes. She seemed tired and looked older than she usually did. A gust of damp cold made Alice peer up the canyon. There were clouds forming ahead, higher, beginning to hide the westernmost peaks before them, and filtering into the higher passes. She had a sense of—in fact thought she could even hear—a blank spot in the circle of natural vibrations that surrounded them. The kind of damping and muffling that accompanies the light falling of new snow.

At the lodge the giant guest lounge, over one hundred feet long, was almost entirely empty. The lights had been lowered so the view would be clearer. Three spectacular sixty-foot-high windows along the back wall gave a truly impressive access to the Tetons by moonlight. Directly below lay Willow Flats, a broad marshy area where it was not uncommon to see as many as fifty moose grazing in the twilight. And beyond, past the irregular edges of Jackson Lake, five or six miles of mountain water reached to the base of Mount Moran. And then the rising mountain, eerie as a watch dial in the moonlight, looking closer than it was, perhaps a fifteen-minute walk, if the swamp didn't look so tricky, and the moose didn't give one legitimate pause. It was because of its height, and the abruptness of its ascent. A huge clump of rock, over twelve and a half thousand feet high, and seeming just as broad. A slightly collapsed sand castle with snow on top, its peak ringed by permanent glaciers. The Triple Glaciers on the north, Falling Ice Glacier southeast of the summit, and almost due east, shining directly at the lodge, was Skillet Glacier. Skillet Glacier, where a plane had buried itself in the mountain and still remained, locked in the ice. But no one was looking, no one was worshiping in this temple dedicated to the mountains. The great hall was quiet. Interest was directed elsewhere. The noise echoed up the broad stone stairway from the lobby, where the people were that night.

The guests were talking to guests and staff was talking with staff. Some vaguely sensed standard of position, on the one hand, and loyalty, on the other, kept them from talking to each other. And there were more people there than an hour before. Some had left, but more had arrived, hearing different sides of the same story over and over as they mingled, trying to sort the contradictory and overlapping images into a single satisfying picture. While the rangers tried to assemble the most accurate story, the spectators persisted in building the most exciting one.

Bill Shaw was close to finishing. It had taken longer than he had expected, but sometimes that was a good sign. There had been times when he had known just what he wanted to do and where he was going, when some minor discrepancy had arisen to delay and divert him. And irritate him. And in the end sometimes it had been that little annoyance which had been the real clue, shown the real direction, and he would have ignored it if he had persisted in his original plan. But you never knew. It could also turn out that it was merely the inconsequential pain in the ass that it appeared to be.

First it was the two rangers who had been working the lobby. They had shown their diligence by finishing it before he could get away. Or Chuck had. Ryner was back stolidly at his post. Bill had hoped to leave it to them, not to have to deal with the cackling crowd of doctors and their wives, or even with the more discreetly murmuring ring of employees that fringed the room. But he had been undone by his helper and had to sift through his findings. And yield to his pride in his work. Chuck insisted he personally interrogate the prize witnesses he had located, the way some people insist you immediately open a present they have brought.

"I think we finally got something with these photos," Chuck had said, trying to remain low-key and professional.

"What've you got?"

Chuck handed him four photos.

"There were only three of them, weren't there?"

"One of them is probably a false ID," Chuck admitted readily.

He handed Shaw the list of those who had identified the photos. Shaw studied it for a moment, wondering what to do, how to break it to him so it would be most useful. "Where did you interrogate these people?" he finally asked. Chuck pointed to a small table with a bunch of chairs around it off to one side. "And you just had a crowd of them come over and sit around and go through the snaps?" Shaw asked. Chuck nodded, more warily now, intuitively recognizing the menace concealed in the Socratic method.

"That's what I thought. You see"—Shaw held up the list—"the people who identified the same photos tended to have the same family names. Like husbands and wives. And God knows who else in their party. . . . Now if a bunch of friends or family are all looking over each other's shoulders and telling each other, 'That looks like him, Charlie,' then they tend to all see it that way. And to pick the same photos. These are contaminated judgments. That means they weren't made independently. They may have something to them, but I'd bet you, human nature being what it is, they are worthless." He looked down at the papers Chuck had given him so he wouldn't have to see the hurt expression on his face.

"In the future, please isolate the person looking at the photos. It'll take longer that way, and I know you're eager to get going, and I appreciate that, but that way you will at least know what you got when you get something. Understand?"

Chuck nodded.

And then someone else remembered that the information hostess had been patiently waiting, as asked, and could talk to him if he was ready. He had half-hoped to avoid that, too. In fact, he realized, not for the first time, there were a lot of people he didn't care to talk to. He was basically a private person, who liked to be left alone, and who accepted the fact he was intolerant of many "types," as he called them. But he often had to ignore his personal preferences to do his job properly, and he tried to keep them from interfering.

She was at her small desk in the left rear of the lobby. She almost never sat there. It was mostly a place to keep her things. Usually she circulated through the lobby trying to spread charm and helpfulness, to diffuse an image of the lodge as warm and attractive and attentive to its guests' needs. She was twenty and had been voted The Apple of Apple Valley back home only a year before. With that, plus her looks, plus her personality (personality plus!), she was entitled to spend her summers at the resort showing new guests where the reservation desk was, and the toilets and the coffee shop. She carried a clipboard and could locate the time and place of any convention or lodge activity, and she had sign-up sheets for the raft trips. In season she was a prominent lobby feature, a little maraschino cherry in the tall frosty glass of the mountain lodge.

"I understand you spent some time talking to the person with the dog," Bill said to her, half-sitting on the edge of her immaculate desk. He tried to look paternally gruff rather than irritable. But her essential pleasantness seemed to be immune to that degree of subtlety.

"Yes, we talked for quite a while. In fact, I think I might have been the only one she talked to. Is there some way I could help you?" she asked politely, looking quite poised.

"Please tell me all you can remember about this person, from the time of entering, and everything that was said to you. There may be something helpful in that."

"The same things I told the rangers?" she asked.

"I know they already have your statement," he explained patiently. "But there are still a lot of things we don't know. So maybe if we go over it again really carefully we'll be able to find something we didn't see before that will make it clearer. I have no way of knowing beforehand how useful it will be, but I would appreciate your trying." He spoke slowly and carefully. It wasn't worth asking the questions if your witness didn't understand them and want to be helpful.

"Well, she was a really striking-looking person. Everyone could see that right away. And when she came in, with that dog and all, everyone just sort of stared at her. It wasn't very polite, but they really couldn't help it. But she didn't seem to mind at all. I really admired how self-possessed and charming she was, with a whole room of people staring at her, you know. I would love to be able to do that as well. Really." She showed him with her face how earnest she was.

"Just how did she look?"

"She looked like a movie star. At least that's what I thought at first, even though I didn't recognize her from anything. And I thought she acted like one, too. You don't learn that kind of elegance just hanging around some bar."

He suppressed a sigh by pulling in his lips and looking out thoughtfully from under his brows. He had been asking about the clothing, actually, but he let it go. It was probably already in the report somewhere. "How did you two get together?"

"Well, she was just standing there. Right in the

middle of the floor, but down at the other end, by the doors, you know. Like there was a spotlight on her, I thought. And she would just look around with this really charming expression on her face. And then she would pat that beautiful dog. She was wearing long gloves with a few rings on over them. She was really, you could say, overdressed for this place, but she carried herself so beautifully that it made everyone else look a little dumpy, if you know what I mean." She looked down at her own simplified cowgirl outfit, her regular uniform of boots, beige skirt, and vest over a pert little blouse.

"And how was it that you two got talking?" he asked pleasantly, as if he weren't actually repeating himself.

"Well, I'm supposed to help people feel at home here. If someone looks lost, or like they might need something, I'm supposed to go up to them and ask. Or even if I just have an intuition. They give me a lot of freedom to make those kinds of decisions, although sometimes Mr. Burnell watches me and gives me some tips on the lodge style." He didn't know who Mr. Burnell was. He didn't ask.

"So you went up to her and asked if you could help?"

For an instant she looked offended, as if he had told the punch line of her story. Or was rushing her, not interested in the way she actually saw it. But she was too good-natured to take it to heart. "She said I had a really lovely hotel. I remember that because I wondered if she thought that just because I came up to her that maybe it was actually my place. But more likely she was just being pleasant. Mostly people ask me questions right off. When someone tells me something like that first I know they are really self-possessed and at ease. It's like they actually see you, instead of just what they need, the way most people do when they first come in. With most people they're more likely to give compliments and thanks when they leave rather than when they come in. When they come in they want the toilets first, usually."

"And what did you two talk about, actually?" It slipped out and he was sorry, concerned he might have offended her again, but she seemed to have accepted his manner as his own, rather than something to take personally.

"Shall I tell it to you one thing at a time, as it happened, or did you have some other way that you'd like me to do it?" she asked him firmly, meeting his eyes without self-doubt and showing him she could not be bullied. She had three brothers and was quite used to men.

"Please. Just the way you saw it," he acquiesced completely.

"Well, I think she asked me if this was still the Western States Medical Association meeting, and when I said it was, she laughed and said they did certainly look like doctors' wives. I was surprised because it seemed like a petty remark from a person like her, but it was actually the only cutting thing she said. Everything else couldn't have been more pleasant. And even that didn't sound so bad, the way that she said it. She had a really beautiful voice. Like a singer." She thought for an instant. "Maybe a little like Carol Channing. Do you know who she is?" He nodded.

"I don't remember the order of all the things we talked about after that. We stood there for a few minutes, just talking, and then she left. But I can give you the idea of it. . . ." She looked at him to see if that met with his approval. He nodded again, not quite trusting his voice yet.

"Well, she said she loved the floor. It's a new floor, you know. She talked like that: she loved this and she loved that. Really enthusiastic, you know. And she asked if it was made out of pressed sawdust, or something like that. I really didn't know the answer to that one, but I remember her saying that they did such wonderful things with Masonite these days. And she said she loved my little vest. That made me feel good. I had been thinking it was a little tiresome, wearing it night after night. But it's the end of the season, and there's no point in worrying about that. And it really has been a super job." Her enthusiasm triumphed again.

Bill said nothing this time and she found her own way without help. "And I talked to her, too. It was a regular conversation that went back and forth. I told her that I liked her dog. It was really beautiful and looked like it had just had a wash and set. And she had a beautiful braided leather leash for it, too, that looked very expensive. And I told her I liked her hair. She had the greatest wig on. It was just magnificent. She told me it was one hundred percent natural hair, every bit of it. And she wished she could actually take it off right there and show it to me, but she didn't think that would make it. Not right there in the lobby with everyone looking at us. I thought that showed that she had a real sense of humor, as well as being poised, and that is very important."

She paused and thought. He left her her space and after a minute she said, "Only one more thing

that I can think of, before she thanked me and
said she had to leave now. It slipped my mind because I couldn't make sense out of it. She said
what a nice place this would be for an FFA convention. I asked her if she meant the Future
Farmers of America and she actually laughed and
said that I was very cute and she had very much
enjoyed speaking with me. I thought that was a
very nice thing to say. A lot of people don't appreciate it when you're helpful. They think they have
it coming because they're guests, which they do,
actually, but still . . ." She looked self-absorbed for
the first time. "I mentioned it to Mr. Burnell," she
complained, "but he didn't seem to think it was
such a big deal. Which actually makes me wonder
where he's at."

"Just another question or two and we'll be done.
Did you have any feeling at any time that she
might have actually been a man?"

"You mean a man all dressed up in a woman's
clothing?" she asked. "That's not the first time I've
heard that tonight. Some people sure have imagina-
tions, that's all I could say to that one. Now you've
made me remember something else, just saying
that. She asked me one time where the little girl's
room was, just in case she had to, you know, because if she did she sure didn't want to tinkle in
the middle of the lobby." Her laugh rang bell-like
and delighted across the lobby, and people turned
to look at them. "Can you imagine a man saying
something like that?" she asked him, and she
laughed again at the thought of it.

Bill Shaw was headed for the relief of the cool
night and a quiet solitary drive to Moose head-

quarters when one of the rangers, Chuck, it was, caught him before the door again. "They found a dog that matches the description. On the road down near Moose. Described it as a 'dumb-blond-looking' dog."

"They all look like that," he snapped.

"Shall I tell them to bring it to the pound, then?"

"No, it's probably the only one like that in the state, damn it. Tell them to hold it for me at the station. I'm on my way. Tell them I don't want to talk to anyone right now."

"They said to tell you that the dog has definitely been identified as a male," the man told him with the same serious expression.

Is he putting me on? Has he been putting me on all along? Bill wondered as he left, shaking his head a bit, under his breath, as it were.

Going to the Cowboy Bar for a drink that night was not a single act but a distinct series of stages. The mob at the door reminded Norman of bees at a hive, in their sounds, in their movements, and in the jagged electrical vibes they energized. A stern young woman at the door checked ID's and let them squeeze in, a few at a time, in some rough approximation of the fire regulations. He joined the crowd of tourists and wranglers waiting on the plank sidewalk outside. Just another busy bee, eager to turn over his pollen to the bar and get a glass of honey in return. The streets were full of people wandering from one bar to another. There were lines outside of them all. This was the start of what was called "cocktail hour" in Jackson, the off season from Labor Day to Memorial Day, when if you didn't like the snow, and if you were tired of making love, then all that was left was to drink.

Inside the bar a few minutes later he found the place to be mostly bodies. But they seemed suspended in some thick fluid and when he pushed firmly and steadily they slowly moved and let him through. It was through that dense flesh-honey that he waded to the bar. It was covered three to four thick, further than he could reach over heads and shoulders to order or collect a drink. He wanted a little corner for himself somewhere that would let him rest and mellow out and sip beer. The women wouldn't be through before tomorrow noon at the earliest. And he would be there by then, just in case, but knowing them, they would stop on the way to look at flowers and the view, cook some nice little lunch in a glade, and arrive refreshed and pleased with themselves somewhere in the afternoon. "It seemed a shame to rush when everything was so beautiful," they would say. Which was quite true.

So he expected a leisurely morning in the mountains even after he arrived at the Teton campgrounds on the other side of the pass to wait for them. It was the deepest he could drive in to meet them from the west, a small, dead-end road ending in a campground in the Targhee National Forest. And then a leisurely drive up through Idaho to Canada. (Where Ruth could finally relax and call home.) And then west, to the Coast, and back down to San Francisco, excited and refreshed by their "vacation" in the Canadian woods. After all that planning and waiting there was little more to wait for. It was time to start enjoying the present. First things first, he decided practically.

The only possible access to the bar was at the service area. There the buzzing was the most ferocious, and it looked as if you could be stung by one of the waitresses in black leotards if you weren't careful. But he decided to take his chances. "Beer!" he said when he caught a bartender's eye, projecting the shape of the word more than the sound. And he stood there, sipping for several minutes, grateful for the cold bite in his throat, yielding to the shoves of the waitresses as they pushed by to place their orders, ignoring their irritated looks. It was everyone for himself tonight. He understood their problems, but they didn't understand his. They would all have to compromise, he decided, and held his ground so he could order again in a minute.

And then, just as he was beginning to feel something like carbonation cheerfully circulating in his blood, the clouds opened up. A beam of light arced down and selected his head as a resting place for its aura, and he was content. The saddle right next to him emptied and no one in the mob had noticed it. He simply hopped onto it and sipped his beer with even greater pleasure, sitting backward, facing the rump, so to speak, scanning the crowd and leaning back, elbows on the bar, checking the stock with the satisfied face of a wealthy rancher. It was soothing entertainment, and quite enough for him after the evening's excitement.

Several slow beers later Norman was pleasantly drifty, letting his mind wander as undisciplined and casual as his eye. Someone was yelling in his ear, an irritating noise focused for some reason at him, and before he could try to understand he felt the crashingly heavy jolt of a drunken hand on his back. "Bobby, Bobby," the man repeated. "Oh, am I glad to see you again. I've been just the shits. Someone stole my dog, can you believe it? I'm practically in a daze." He had a fresh tequila sunrise in his hand and he squeezed over against Norman's leg to get out of the service space. "If you hadn't been right here I never would have seen you. It's so crowded. And I really need a shoulder to cry on. Beardsley and I were so close we were practically intimate. I said 'practically' now. By the way, what happened to you last night? You left early."

The White Swallow. Was that only last night? The thought disoriented him a bit. He didn't actually remember the man. He just remembered something about him. His mind flashed instinctively to his Trick Book, with its neat columns labeled Bar, Name, Address, Inches, Like to Do, and the Score, with ratings from one to ten. It wouldn't be the first time he'd had to slip off for a minute to glance at it to be sure about whom he was talking to. But he hadn't brought the book this trip. And he would just have to glide over and around the name thing.

"I met a trick and split," Norman said. "I really made a sow of myself." He noticed that the man's brown hair had a fine layering of water droplets on it. "Your hair's wet," he said, feeling his back start to tighten, in spite of the beer. That was where he always felt it first, in his back.

"It's wet out there." The man pointed toward the street. "The perils of barhopping. But it's getting late so I'm going to snuggle down here until closing. Only have a little while to dry off my outsides and wet down my insides, before I have to go out there again."

"Raining hard?"

"Not so bad, down here. My, look at that one. Good show. Big thumbs and a fine chunk of nose. All the signs are favorable."

"Come over from Idaho Falls, did you?"

"More or less," he answered coyly. "You wouldn't tell me your secrets, so why should I tell you mine? Isn't this place a trip? Way out West, where bad men are hung good."

"How was Teton Pass?"

"Not closed yet, but it's always the first to go, you know. That reminds me, Bobby baby, if that's really your name. You're so fuckin' mysterious you'd think you were the fuckin' Prince of Wales," he said resentfully. "That pass may close before the night's out, and I'm in no condition to drive anyway. Couldn't you let me crash with you tonight? With all these people in town there won't be a motel room anywhere." He looked pleadingly, checking Norman's face carefully for a flicker of interest. Without glancing down Norman could feel a hand. The contact was light, and could almost pass for accidental, if the insinuation in the touch weren't so heavy.

"I think we can work something out," he answered, "but you're going to have to clean up your act for a while. I mean it, be really cool!" He said it seriously, looking him in the eye so he would understand he meant it. The hand withdrew, the warm spot turned quickly colder. "I play it straight here. I have a job and I want to keep it. If I have to worry about you messing me up you won't be any fun at all. Understand?"

"You can trust me completely, Bobby. Don't worry about a thing. And as a token of your good faith, I want you to tell me a secret. Just a little one. Something you feel you can trust me with, so I'll know I can trust you too. Please?" he pleaded.

"When we get to my place we can play all sorts of games," he promised. "There's no way I'm going to tell you anything here. You're drunk and the next thing you'll be standing on the bar and singing it to the crowd. So you'll just have to wait."

He looked briefly hurt at being refused, but recouped by thinking of a counterdemand. "Then let's both have a drink to Beardsley, the most beautiful Afghan in all Idaho. Two sunrises," he called to a bartender who was shaking something that sounded like pebbles in a can. And even as he twisted all the way around to the bar he kept one hand firmly on Norman's arm, fixing him in space.

"Make those doubles, please," Norman suddenly called over his head.

His friend turned back, looking surprised. Then pleased. "Attaboy," he smiled. "Well," he beamed, "where we going?"

"Huh?"

"You'll have to show me if you don't tell me, so what's the big secret?"

"Okay. You win," Norman agreed good-naturedly. He leaned closer and bent next to the man's ear. "Flagg Ranch. I'm a boatman at Flagg Ranch," he confided with relish.

"You?"

"Why not?" He looked offended. They laughed and the man banged him on the back again.

"Well, you don't have to worry about me."

"Don't you think I know that? But listen, we'll have to be very cool. No noise. And you'll have to leave early." The man sulked. "I could meet you for breakfast," Norman assured him, "but you can't hang around. Listen, then, are you sure we can't go back to your place? I could drive over and meet you there. Then you could sleep late, and be comfortable, and all. It might be much better."

"Noooo, I'm too tired to drive back now. And too tanked. And there's the snow. And the roadblocks. It's too much to cope with tonight."

"Roadblocks too? You poor dear. Were they looking for perverts?"

"Hardly. Probably somebody escaped from prison or something."

"Yeah? What prison?"

"I don't know. I just said probably. Listen, how do you want to do this?"

"I don't want to be seen leaving this place with you," Norman insisted, the solemn voice of reason. "So we'll have to meet."

"I have some poppers in my car. Why don't we meet there?"

"Okay. Where you parked?"

"Three blocks south, on this street. The one right outside. Black Mercedes."

"Okay." Norman calculated for a minute. "I had to park way the hell out of town on the road east. It'll take me five to ten minutes to get there and a bit to get back. Why don't you finish your drink and then take it slow to your car, and I should be there just about the same time you are."

"Why don't I just give you a lift to your car?"

"You don't understand how it is, do you?" Norman demanded, his voice beginning to rise in irritation. The man looked cowed, for the minute anyway. The longer the better, Norman thought. They blinked the lights in the bar to signal that the

2:00 A.M. closing was approaching. "There. We couldn't have timed it better. Now relax and enjoy yourself and finish your drink, and I'll see you in ten or fifteen minutes," he commanded. "Here. Finish this too. Get you nice and loose." And he pushed his own glass, two-thirds full, toward him also. He gave him an instant of intense, deep, eyeball-to-eyeball contact, something he could make anything out of he wanted, and left.

Outside he turned north and hurried around the corner, west, and then north again, checking several times over his shoulder, and stopped by a small, dark pizza parlor. The van was parked in front. He got in, fired up, and hurried out of town, taking the highways west, without waiting an instant for the engine to warm up.

Monday 1:07 A.M.

Back at Moose headquarters things had gone smoothly. It had taken very little time to set the roadblocks, outline the search patterns, shape up the fundamentals. They were working from a position of strength now, using familiar tools and knowledge, and they worked efficiently and welcomed the opportunity to be active. Then came a lull.

It was too dark and too early to do much more. Earlier than he had thought, only around 1:00 A.M. Something could open up at any moment, but Bill was sure they were just settling in for a wait of several hours at least. He felt he was starting to get a little stale just sitting there, talking over the same theories with the same people. He was too charged up to take a nap, which probably would have been the best thing. No, the second best thing. He checked the clock again. It wasn't *that* late, he decided.

Bill picked up the phone and turned partway around toward the wall, shielding himself a bit and indicating this was a private conversation. He counted the rings, trying to guess what was happening at the other end. Five, he counted. "Hi, did I get you up?" he asked softly. "Well, I'm tired and

I'm not. It's the usual story, don't you know. . . .
Things are settling down over here and I thought
I'd like to get away for a little while. Could I drop
over for an hour or so? . . . Fine. See you in a few
minutes."

After the call he sat back in his chair to relax
and clear his head before leaving. He sighed and
noticed his shoulders didn't drop because a knot of
muscle at the back of his neck seemed to be holding them up. He was relieved that everything had
gone pleasantly on the phone. He looked forward
to jumping into bed for half an hour, getting a
back rub too if he could, being able to come back
and start fresh again.

"I'm going out for an hour or so," Bill told the
man at the next desk. "Call me if anything comes
up. Here's the number." He put a strip of paper by
the man's desk blotter. The man slid it underneath
where he would be sure to have it. He didn't look
at the number since he already knew what it was.
Bill glanced around once, nodded to someone, and
then left. He took his official car even though it
was only a five-minute walk. If something broke
open he wanted to be back in less than five minutes.

Diane answered the door wearing only rubber
shower sandals and a faded plaid flannel bathrobe.
Neither of them said anything, but she held the
door back and he stepped in. When the door was
shut he hugged her and felt his body comforted
and mildly stimulated by the warm contact with
her full up the front. He held her until there was
nothing left in his mind but the feel of her against
him. Then he reached for the knot which held her
bathrobe closed.

She put her hand over his, stopping him. "Mike's here," she said, with a lowered voice.

Bill was instantly annoyed. "Why didn't you tell me?"

"Because I wanted to talk to you. I was glad you called."

"Talk?" Bill's voice showed his exasperation without growing loud enough to be overheard. "Don't you know it's past one o'clock in the morning? What time is this to talk?"

"Would you like a cup of coffee?" she asked without responding to his anger. It was that or leave, he knew. He followed her into the kitchen.

The kitchen was a cheerful yellow, but it looked strange with the windows blacked by the night. Silently Diane heated water and poured it over the crystalline coffee. Bill spent the time wanting to forget that his plans had been frustrated yet once more, trying to relax and refresh himself in spite of how things were.

"I wanted to talk to you again," she finally said. "I don't think you heard me before."

He knew instantly what she meant. And he was further annoyed, because he thought he *had* heard her before. This insistence seemed like nagging. "Look, Diane, you know we made an agreement. We agreed that the only way we could ever get together was to leave all this at the office. That was a good agreement. Now I'm tired. I've been at this all night and I came here to get away from it."

"I'm sorry this is hard on you, Bill, but this isn't an ordinary night. These aren't ordinary things that have happened and I think it would be foolish to stick to our rule. It doesn't apply. Now I've got something I want to tell you, something I've given a lot of thought, and I'm determined to try."

He looked down at the table, tired and bothered, but he didn't leave. So she launched into her explanation, not raising her voice so she wouldn't wake Mike, more slowly and calmly now than earlier that evening, because it just drove him up a tree to deal with someone who was hysterical. She had thought it all out. After he called she had summarized her arguments, putting them in logical order that climbed directly, like a stairway, to her conclusion.

Bill sat back with his coffee and tried to rest. He had no heart for an argument, and no interest in explanations. Well-meaning people were always trying to tell him what to do, how to do his work. He had long ago given up trying to explain that his world was different from what they imagined it to be. Forget the sex. It would have been beautiful just to get the back rub.

After a minute Diane sensed, and then saw, the clouds across his eyes. Eyes that were beginning to puff without sleep, facial lines looking a little deeper in the strong kitchen light. All right, she thought. All right. Maybe tomorrow. I'll be angry, but it's too much trouble now. We're both tired. Poor old folks, she thought sympathetically.

She had a sudden moment of clarity, a perspective on it all, and it saddened her. These two nice people couldn't make each other happy. For he *was* a nice person, in addition to being many other things. But if this was how it was going to go, it was clearly impossible. And they would each lose, regretfully, one more hope of comfort.

She gave up explaining and reached out, patted

him on the arm, and rested her hand there, aware of the two of them, her in her old bathrobe, him in his wrinkled uniform, weary in the kitchen in the middle of the night.

It was a minute before he seemed to realize she had stopped talking. They both sat there, looking at her hand on his arm, thinking their own thoughts. Then he patted her hand gently with his, thanked her formally for the coffee, and headed back to work.

At the end, the channel of Cascade Canyon came against a wall which extended to the crest, running thin and sharp along the top of the range. The creek divided there. The trail divided too, spreading into an open "Y" with the arm running almost north and south. The North Fork was the popular trail. The southerly path led only deeper in and higher up. Eventually, though, for those who persisted, it worked its way through the range and down the other side. That was their way through the night.

Looking back down the canyon Alice could see how smoothly the giant glaciers carved, glaciers which many times dominated that landscape and which, inevitably, would return to rule again. It only took a relatively small change in the climate, she knew. Snow accumulated. More snow fell in the winter than melted the following summer, and gradually the great grinding force of glaciers took weight. Canyons which were sharp, narrow gorges were bored out at the bottom to leave level, open floors and smooth walled sides which were quite steep.

The South Fork, the path they took, climbed several thousand feet over the next three and a half miles in a series of giant steps. They too were glacial, a glacial staircase. Short, wide valleys ended in almost vertical stone cliffs which they climbed by switchbacks. The valleys were little meadows, easy to walk through, the grasses and flowers slowly being covered by the early snow. They had passed through several forests, white-bark pine and spruce. Somewhere nearby grew the largest known whitebark pine in the world, some-where in one of the dense groves they had bisected as they followed the river path. And just a few miles further along the trail, as they continued to climb higher into the mountains, the same trees grew again, or perhaps survived without really growing, as small shrubs, stunted by the altitude.

It was right near the tree line that the trail split once more, although it was not that evident with several inches of snow accumulated by now, unless you knew it was there. To the left was part of a trail which no longer went through. It was unsafe because it ran along crumbling rock at the base of a very steep wall. Almost no one went there any-more. If Ruth dies I can drag her body there and no one would find her until the thaw in July. And maybe not even then. It was an ugly, practical thought. She continued to watch her friend, to be aware of any chance to help.

Ruth knew they were surrounded by mountains. The mountains moved with them as they hiked, the way the moon sometimes seemed to keep pace alongside her van, and as they climbed higher and had a larger view, the mountains around them seemed bigger, not smaller. But she was not inter-ested, she seldom looked. These were incidental impressions from occasionally raising her head because her neck muscles demanded it every so often.

She pictured Alice constantly craning to look at them, her eyes bright, her face rapturous. She herself hated mountains, she realized. It was a new attitude, only a few hours old, but it had a solid, permanent feeling to it already. What she saw was what she stepped on. She looked down at her feet and at a small area a few steps ahead. That was her world and had been for half the night. She tried to keep her mind in that small space also, with intermittent success. "Step," she told herself. "Don't think, just step."

Some people wear bells, she thought. It was supposed to be extra bad to surprise a bear. If you wore a bell, just a little one, it could hear you coming. Alice had said she would never wear a bell in the woods. She prized her solitude too much. Fuck her. Let her get eaten by a bear. She had no right to risk other people's lives just because . . . The bears didn't always run away when they knew you were there. People had been eaten by bears in national parks before. Only a few years ago. Women. Only women. In Glacier and in Yellowstone. They said it may have been because they had their periods. The bears smelled their blood and came to get them. Just like they would come to get a rabbit. But it was only the grizzlies you had to worry about. Alice said there weren't likely to be any on this trail. But then she wasn't menstruating fresh warm blood, leaving a smear of scent in the canyon which led right to her soft, white belly. She pictured teeth sinking into her flesh. As if there were no barrier. As if it weren't her. Just like it

was a piece of melon, or something. A hunk of
something to be eaten without hesitation or regret.
The way a bear would see it.

Now the frights came as regularly as the
cramps. She didn't know which tired her more. A
stick on the trail, black and twisted against the
snow, was a snake. An instant later her mind told
her that snakes liked warm places. They were
holed up somewhere waiting for summer, dream-
ing of hot flat rocks. But that was already after her
nerves had been, again, strummed by some giant
hand, and another hot spurt of her precious energy
had been spilled generously, and without her con-
sent, into her bloodstream. A bush was a bear. A
rock was falling. The earth was shifting. She could
not stop the recurrent experience of calamity no
matter how strictly she disciplined her mind. She
did not tell Alice. It would worry her and there was
nothing she could do.

At the last rest Alice had fussed sweetly over
her, patting and encouraging her. Ruth knew it
was "sweet," cynically remembering the signs from
a past existence. But it didn't feel sweet. It didn't
help. Alice had rearranged her pack, adjusting the
straps like a sailor tuning the rigging. Mostly because she was frustrated and there was so little she
could do. Ruth had continued to walk as before,
bent over and staring at the space just in front of
her toes, the only space she believed in, the next
place she had to put her foot. The cramps in her
belly didn't let her straighten up all the way. And
in a world where sensation was equivalent to pain,
she wanted as small a universe as possible.

But she didn't have to see to feel. Her heart had
become irregular. She could recognize the strug-

gling of a small animal in danger. In her chest.
Perhaps it was suffocating, trying to reach air. Too
late. There was not enough. She never got enough
anymore. No matter how much she breathed she
was always behind, always struggling to catch up.
And her head still hurt. She would take some
aspirin when they stopped. Because they would
have to stop, she was beginning to realize. *She*
would have to stop. She tried to think about pain
instead. Her stomach didn't bother her, if she
didn't pay attention to it. But further down there
was a hot, runny feeling, a slippery sensation that
told her she was slowly losing her grip on her
bowels. It was the same with the bladder. Once you
let go you had to do it over and over again. It was
the first time that you could hold out the longest.
She could still hold out longer. It wasn't time yet.

It was getting colder, much colder. The snow
continued steadily and as they came more directly
under the clouds the moonlight was more completely absorbed. She wished the moon would come
back, as if it were the moonlight which was giving
them warmth. At least it was a comfort to have it
there. It diffused just minimally through the
clouds. Their eyes had adjusted so that they could
still make their way along the night trail, but now
with ever-increasing difficulty. The snow had its
own glow. But it was not as if there were any light,
and she found the experience stifling. And still no
word from Alice. Quiet, self-sufficient, self-absorbed Alice. The wood nymph. The girl scout. It
was just as well, If she had opened her mouth at
the wrong moment Ruth knew she would have
used up the last bit of energy lashing at her. Just

to have the release. But Alice seemed to sense it, and gave her plenty of room.

Everything was getting worse. They had just climbed and were now trudging across a flat. When she glanced up, looking ahead, there was a feeling of marching straight at a wall, something you would smack into. In some places the switchbacks were visible, the trail not completely hidden by the snow and dark. But before they got there and mindlessly began to climb again, Alice stopped her with her hand. They stood together like that for a moment, Ruth not asking, both of them just breathing. "That's a tough one," Alice finally said. "But it's the end of the worst." They both looked up, measuring the height in pain rather than distance. "On top is Hurricane Pass. That's the crest of our climb." The top wasn't clear from where they stood. They were too near the base, and the rock face arced back away from them, concealing its limits.

"I think there used to be a sign up there: 'Leaving Grand Teton National Park, Entering Targhee National Forest.' After that we're out of the park. Still very much in the mountains," she laughed ironically, "but out of the park, at least. And then it's pretty much a piece of cake. Mostly downhill, I think, all the rest of the way to the campgrounds." Alice wiped a runny nose on her sleeve.

Ruth nodded. "That's great," she told herself, but it sounded like polite conversation, nothing very sincere. She felt more of a rush when she told herself she would stop there. She would tell Alice she had to stop and they would just find a nice little place off the trail and flop for a while. Until she felt better. She had to. It was safe enough. No one

was around, or was likely to be. Over that crest
and they would be out of sight of the trail. And
out of the park. She wasn't sure if that had any
real advantage. But the further they went the less
likely anyone would connect them with the events
behind them. In that way it was a concrete mea-
sure of progress. And even at a time when getting
away seemed less important than surviving, it still
felt good.

They stood for another minute, gathering
strength, Alice solidly planted with her hand still
on Ruth's shoulder. Insisting on her presence,
diffusing some of her energy, sharing. Alice's voice
had not irritated her. On the contrary, it had been
some kind of relief. Silence can make you a little
crazy, Ruth thought. She could feel again what a
lovely person Alice was, and her nightmares were
thin and pale for the moment.

"Okay. I'll go ahead, for a while." Alice led off,
keeping it slow and steady.

Just over the top. And then down the west slope,
into some sheltered nook for rest and healing,
Ruth told herself. That much and no more. She
had been playing that game for some time, using
it like a carrot to draw herself forward a few more
steps. "If you go there, you can rest," she would
tell herself. "Only to there," she would nag as she
went along. And then when she got there she
would tell herself she had been mistaken. She had
really meant there, a little further on. How silly
she had been to think it meant here. There. But the
game was worn out. It would really have to be
there.

She had been trying to create excuses to stop,
she realized. Somewhere in the last hour she had

begun assuming they would be caught. It was a discouraging, energy-sapping thought. It made struggling seem foolish. An empty gesture. A vanity. Norman had been caught at the roadblock, she decided. And they were going through all this for nothing. The police would be waiting for them at the top. No, that was too inviting a picture, too pleasant. It meant they could stop there. They would be waiting at the end of the trail. After the two of them battled all the way through, there, at the last steps, rounding the final bend, they would walk into a clearing, too tired even to protest, to deny, and the police would be waiting and take them. Chuckling at their exhaustion and wasted effort.

Or if the police were not there, if no one were there, if Norman wouldn't say anything and the police had to figure it out for themselves, then they would be waiting for her at her home. Two of them, sitting across the street in a parked car, chewing gum and reading newspapers. Not an unpleasant job, waiting until she showed up. One or the other would go out for coffee and sandwiches regularly. Otherwise they would stay stretched out there, feet up on the seats, making themselves comfortable, one in the front and one in the back, passing time and collecting their pay. Until she came home. Could she get Posey and make it to Canada? Or Mexico? Where was it safe? she tried to remember. Was it Brazil? Why hadn't they checked this all out?

They had been prepared for snow. "You don't climb in the Tetons and not prepare for snow," Alice had said. Not where the easier trails were likely to be snow-covered until the middle of July.

And the higher passes and glacial trails had snow
and ice all year round. Not where it could snow
any time of the year, and regularly did. It was not
uncommon for people to die in these mountains.

They had already zipped on their gaiters a while
back. These were sleeves of nylon which fitted over
the tops of their shoes and up the calf. A strap
went under the arch to hold it down, and a draw-
string at the top sealed it tight. They kept socks
and feet dry in the snow. It couldn't fall into the
tops of their boots and melt there and run down
in.

And now they unhooked their ice axes and
leaned on them as they climbed. Miserly as they
had been with weight and space, realizing they
would have to drag every ounce over the mountains using vital energy, they had still decided on
the ice axes. Almost another two pounds, and a
sharp and awkward bulk, and still they had them.
"There are times when you just aren't safe if you
don't have one," Alice had explained regretfully,
making the decision for them as Ruth had looked
at the implements with distaste.

Reaching from the wrist to the ground, the proper height to function as a walking stick, a prop, a
third foot, when grasped at the head. It was one of
the three points that were needed, when one had to
be careful to always keep at least two points down
on snow or ice at all times. Her two feet were the
other two points. When walking on a snowy slope
one never picked up a foot without first putting
the ax end down firmly. The butt of the wooden
handle ended in a sharp metal point. Always two
points to rest, or lean on, or stabilize with. And if you
happened to slip, if you started to slide down and

to pick up speed on the lubricated incline, the ice ax was almost your only hope. Often the last factor deciding whether you would be injured or killed. It was your brake. You fell across it, digging the pick end into the crust, pressing your weight on it, hoping it would hold, stop, before you slid over some edge and dropped.

They used them now, as they climbed. But this was mostly new snow. There was only occasionally a firmer layer of base underneath, the packed residue of an earlier snowfall. Where the point came into a section of hardpack, it dug and held. It gave momentary support and a little lift to the weary legs from the unused arm muscles. But where the point found no base, it took back the tiny dab of energy which had been saved, and more. Where the point went into soft new fluff, or a bit of flattened wet grass growing from a crack, or merely onto the smooth surface of the rock itself, it skittered out, pulling them off-balance, often bringing them down, pack and all, slipping to their knees or sides, having to climb back up with the extra fifty pounds on their backs, always thankful they hadn't slipped from some ledge. Always resentful that more strength had been stolen from them by the unsympathetic terrain. People do this for fun, Ruth thought, permitting herself a wry chuckle. At least she wasn't that crazy. The thought pleased her.

They were beginning to get wet. The falling not only banged her knees, but she could also feel the moisture penetrate her wool pants. Wool was good. It would hold. More or less. But less than comfortable. And getting heavier. The moisture spread through the cotton long johns underneath. They would be less effective. The snow was deeper as they approached the crest, formed into small cornices by the wind which pushed it out of the pass above them.

Ruth was amazed she could still feel relief, but she felt it. The trail was leveling out. Her steps were more forward than upward. There was not the same pressure from lifting the pack each step, the resistance of gravity, the repeated objection of muscles along the tops of her thighs. She stumbled a few steps. The sign was there, nearby, as Alice had said it would be, even though she could not read it. Wind-driven snow stuck to most of its surface. They had made it.

"Around . . ." and she could not go on for the moment. She pointed down with one gloved hand, pointed at the earth she wanted to rest on. ". . . here." Alice seemed to understand. Ruth continued to stagger on, trying to make whatever final progress was necessary before they camped. It was unpleasant in a new way now. The wind beat her face with a crystal whip, the snow lashing. They went on a bit, partly just from momentum, looking bewildered at the land around them.

It was charitable to call it land. Hurricane Pass wasn't like any pass Ruth had known. It was flat and open. Everywhere it was smooth stone. The resting place of still another glacier. A throne where only an ice queen could sit. Nothing more than a quarter-mile of arching stone, the ridge at the top of their trail, which then descended into a similarly smooth stone valley. The snow didn't stick. There were a few drifts, but mostly it was bare. There was no place for it to wedge in. Nothing grew there. There was no need to ask how it got its name. It was horrible.

"This is no good," Alice said, looking around, wincing from the wind and the added cold it brought. "I think we should go back down," she said regretfully.

"All the way back?" Ruth asked, and felt embarrassed that she had revealed her wish. If only it were that simple, she was sure she would do it. And gratefully.

Alice turned her around, back the way they had just come. Giving up any ground when each bit had been taken at such cost seemed so painfully wasteful. They passed the sign again, into the park once more. And over the sloping edge, sliding and stepping, working partway down, Alice keeping a hand on her arm or her pack, to steady and guide her, to control her descent. And then sideways, traversing the slope and abandoning the trampled path they had made on the way up, over the shelter of a promising overhang of snow with a soft-looking bank underneath it.

Ruth hunched there, propped on her ice ax, not looking, letting her pack lie in the snow next to her. Alice spread out a tarpaulin as best she could, trying to shape it into the sheltering curve of the snow and give them a dry place to sit or lie. And then she pulled the Ensolite pads from the packs, unfurling their stiff curls, bending them backward until the foam insulation lay more or less flat on the tarp. That would prevent much of the heat loss to the cold from below. She pulled the sleeping bags from their stuff sacks, fluffing them out to expand the compressed goose down so they regained their insulating air pockets. She unzipped them to use open, as blankets. Ruth looked too tired to crawl into hers right then, even though it would be warmer.

It was only when Ruth sat down that it all hit. Struggling, difficult as it had been, was also a distraction. Now the nausea came rolling over the weakness and the tiredness, and the shortness of breath, and the stomach cramps. And she leaned over the edge of the tarp and vomited. Alice knelt alongside with a supporting arm around her, holding her up. When she was done it was Alice who covered the mess with handfuls of snow, and then washed her face off with a bit more. Ruth really didn't care. She began to whimper, letting everything go, not able to hold anything together anymore.

"It's all right, you'll be all right, you'll be okay," Alice repeated over and over, sounding so worried and unhappy too. "I know you feel awful," she said at one time. "It's altitude sickness, that's all. You'll get better. We'll just stay here until you feel better. You don't have to walk anymore. Just rest. It'll go away after a while. You'll see." But after that she only made soothing sounds, like you would to a child, and held her head in her lap and rocked her back and forth, back and forth. And Ruth moaned her pain into the cold empty canyon.

Monday 5:45 A.M.

Early. Cold and damp. Not exactly an ideal day for a hike, Mike thought as they walked to the car in the predawn drabness. He wasn't enthusiastic about their expedition, but he said nothing to Diane. In fact, he was grateful for some of the ways she pushed him. He got to do much more because of her, much more than he would have if left to his own sporadic enthusiasms. The job itself was the result of her influence. He had said, in passing, that it must be great to spend the summer in the Tetons. And she had taken him up on it, not realizing it was mostly a polite remark, a way of trying to say he thought her job was "interesting," when he couldn't think of what else to call his unconventional aunt's work. He really thought it was rather a strange job for a woman, compared to a normal existence. That same strangeness made him cautious and polite around her. He was actually afraid of provoking one of her unsettling little "talks." And conflict seemed an excuse for her to sit down and engage in face-to-face debate during which she would ask what he felt and say what was on her mind. None of that went on at his house, and he did his best to avoid it here.

But aside from that he felt he would probably be

happy when they were out and moving. He usually was. And this was his last weekend of a fabulous summer. He was already growing nostalgic. Later that day, at the right moment, he planned to be alone for a little while. Then he would go off a ways and say good-bye to the mountains and the valley. It had been a great summer. And now he couldn't wait to watch his parents' faces when they saw he finally had lost some weight.

The '67 VW outside had originally been a pale blue-gray. Now it looked prepared for camouflage. The year before Diane had sanded the rust spots off it and covered the bare places with dabs of dark gray primer. She planned to paint the whole thing soon. But after a time it became more pleasant to like it the way it was rather than expend the energy to change it for purely cosmetic reasons. It ran well. She turned on the lights and drove carefully to Moose headquarters. It was a little before six. If they didn't waste time they could make the trail head just after sunrise. The building gave out light and energy which seemed unnatural at that hour.

The front room, the visitors' information center, was still closed. Behind that were many offices and a large room, brightly lighted and bustling with uniformed and plain-clothed workers. Several new maps had been put up, one a gas-station issue which showed state highways. On it was an accumulation of pushpins, thumbtacks, and even a few straight pins with bits of ribbon tied on, or scraps of torn paper slid on the shafts for visibility. They didn't have the nice little monopoly pieces that big agencies used for this kind of search.

In one corner, hopefully out of the way, a large Afghan lay on the floor, his leash tied to a desk leg.

From time to time he lifted his head and gave out a thin, high sound which was pleading and sad. He also raised his head when anyone walked into the room, looking at them quickly before lying back down between his paws.

Diane stopped to watch them, Mike automatically heeling, waiting for her to lead. Bill Shaw was there, making earnest faces into a telephone he held against his ear with his shoulder, writing and holding down the paper with his large hands. He didn't notice them. There was a cluster of desks in that corner, all pulled over from their normal spacing. Other men talked on telephones, to each other, or leaned back in their swivel chairs and stared at the maps. Everyone was drinking coffee, unconsciously and almost constantly sipping between sentences, cigarettes, and head scratchings.

Someone walked right by them, nodding, and they nodded back. Aside from that only the dog looked their way, now rolling his expressive eyes here and there without turning or lifting his head. Diane looked as serious as they did, almost visibly thinking as she watched the scene. The pins on the maps were spreading, moving outward further and further along the few roads that radiated from the park. Little pins marching along the still dark highways of Wyoming, Utah, Idaho. A voodoo rite. A secret wish to impale some invisible bug which was out there, somewhere, still infuriatingly nowhere.

She resolved whatever had concerned her and continued walking, back to the corner at the other side of the room. The equipment room. She checked out an ice ax from ranger supplies for Mike. He picked one of the right height, measuring from his wrist to the floor, with an eye for a pleasing wood grain in the handle, while she wrote out the slip. And then they left, without a word or another look, watched only by the dog, to drive back to Jenny Lake.

A ranger pushed past them as they went, stepped just inside the door and called out to the room, "Who has the key to the red-top out back?"

"It's on the board."

"It's not on the board."

"Then it's probably Williams. He always puts them in his pocket and walks off."

"Where is he?"

"Don't know. Take another one."

"They're all busy."

"Well, wait then," was the impatient reply. "There'll be another one in a minute. In the meantime bring over some radio messages. Make yourself useful."

Bill Shaw was feeling good. If you had to work, you might as well work hard. Do it. Do it right. And get it over with. In the ideal job you worked until you were finished and exhausted, slept until you were rested, and woke to a fresh, clear day. He had pretty near an ideal job. The planning and execution was going well. Nothing significant had turned up yet, but it was just a matter of time. They had good minds, some of the best men in the area were there, working hard and together, a tough team to beat. This type of work was like that —you kept doing what you knew had to be done, one thing after another, and often nothing showed until suddenly it all broke open. He was consciously very respectful to all the important visitors. He was very polite to the sheriff. He was even deferen-

tial to the FBI man (this was federal property and
they were automatically involved). But that was
because he was in charge. When it was over he
would also thank them profusely and publicly. Not
the other way around. And in the meantime he
listened to all their suggestions like a subordinate.
"An excellent idea," he always agreed. "Yeah, that's
good. But those men are tied up right now, unfortunately. I'll see they get to it just as soon as
they're free," he would promise, regretful that it
couldn't be sooner. They understood. And he understood that he couldn't keep too tight a grip.
They had to earn their pay, too. They needed to
look smart and effective and he cooperated with
them as they did with him.

Even the frustrations were, in a way, enjoyable.
What was the use of having teeth if you didn't get
something tough to chew on now and then? And
like a good cop he had shaped his bite to the piece
of pie he had been served. First things first, he had
decided. There were thousands of people in the
park and the valley this weekend. Unless they
were lunatics, and suicidal to boot, the trio had
changed their clothing and their automobile. Some
link was going to be needed to trace them. The car
was that link. It was somewhere nearby, out of the
park but somewhere still in the valley, almost inevitably abandoned and waiting for them at this very
moment. It was too big to conceal in that terrain
for long. And when they found it there would be,
almost inevitably, something they needed to single
out the people who had been in it. They would find
the car. And the car would find the people.

He had always been amazed at the carelessness
of amateurs, and he had dealt almost exclusively

with amateurs throughout his career in the park.
Because they were willing to shut their eyes to little
things, unpleasant details, they assumed that the
police would too. They failed to take into account
what it meant to be a professional. What it meant
to be painstaking, to examine every detail, to be
willing to do what was necessary even though it
might be boring, difficult, or exhausting. A professional justified his existence through just that.
And if you were the kind of get-rich-quick schemer
who was dodo enough to rob a national park in the
first place, you were not going to be able to understand or anticipate that fact.

Amazingly the kinds of lapses that ended up
snaring the flashy clever types included leaving
credit-card receipts with real names on them
jammed into the crack of the seat after buying gas.
Matchbooks with motel names, places where they
had actually stayed recently and registered under
real names. Or registered under aliases and listed
their real license-plate numbers. Or had forgotten
some item of clothing which could be traced. Or
left still another matchbook there which could be
traced still further back to their origins. Or thrown
away an envelope addressed to them. Or made a
remark to the person at the desk. Or, at very least,
were seen in their normal appearance and could
then be identified from composites. Or . . . There
was a long list to look forward to painstakingly
checking out. And at the very end, if they had any
previous record, there were always the fingerprints.

So the car was their ace. Every time they got another negative report back from the radio operator,
various rangers running the messages from the
comm center just down the hall, the group around

the map asked themselves and each other if the car could have gotten out. No, they agreed. No way. Out of the gate, yes, but never out of the valley.

So the search progressed, carefully, painstakingly, professionally. They listed all the places they thought you could hide a car in the area, blitzed the most likely ones first, chancing a lucky or intuitive hit, and scheduled almost a complete walk-search over the rest of the valley floor. Barns, garages, abandoned farmhouses, canyons, heavy brush. The radio-controlled cars fanned out through the area. It would be light enough for an air search soon and they had great hopes for that. A Piper and a helicopter were at their disposal. Usually flying tourists among the mountains for pictures and thrills, the pilots would be delighted at this unexpected end-of-the-season commission. The first thing Shaw wanted was a low flyover down the length of the Snake. The water was too low this time of year to cover a car, but they were greenhorns and they had ditched it in the dark, so they might not have realized. Or realized only when it was too late. After they had created a new shiny green island with a windshield in three feet of water which had been twelve feet deep during spring runoff.

A note came from communications to the sheriff. Bill watched him put his coffee down and look at the note with annoyance. "What's the matter, Artie?" he asked him.

"Can you believe it? They're already getting backup at Teton Pass." The sheriff had been coordinating the county roadblocks, and keeping in touch with the sheriffs in neighboring counties, monitoring all the highway input.

"Early risers," Bill said, and they both looked mildly disgusted that some travelers might want to get a jump on the great crowd which would spill out of the bowl of Jackson Hole all that day. They enjoyed pretending that if the world weren't so obviously full of dingdongs then no one would be on the road that morning but the three they wanted. "Can they handle it?"

"For a while," the sheriff answered resignedly. This was the biggest weekend of the whole year and everyone would be leaving that day. If the arteries they had blocked to a trickle were kept tied off as the crowd flow got under way, there would be a backup which could make more trouble than it would resolve. They risked a highway hemorrhage. A throughway thrombosis. For the next few hours the sheriff would be constantly in touch with the critical spots, assessing how much tie-up could be managed, and then call off the roadblock and release the flow at the last possible moment.

"What're you hearing?"

Bill shrugged. "Yellowstone's quiet."

"They wouldn't be that stupid."

"You're right. Even stupidity has limits. But why should we have all the fun? Besides, if someone stole one of their geysers. I'd be the first to volunteer to sniff all the cars that passed through here. You know, looking for that fart smell they have . . . And what may I do for you?" he asked with mock sweetness as the FBI man came over to his desk.

"Have you checked the airport?"

"You mean takeoffs?"

"Yeah, that too. But even the possibility of something unauthorized. I was wondering whether a helicopter might get in here and take them out, and if it did, whether traffic control would be monitoring it. Or even the possibility of landing a small plane on a deserted stretch of road or in a field."

Bill thought it unlikely, for a number of reasons. "Sharp. Real sharp." He gave Artie an impressed look. "Hey!" he snapped to a ranger who was walking by, headed for the urn to refill his cup. "Have radio call traffic control at the airport and check out landings and leavings since early last night. Especially helicopters and small planes. You've been here all night, you know what's going on. And hurry!" He rushed the man a touch to show respect for the agent's idea. "You might just have something there," he said to the agent.

"I know it sounds kind of James Bondish," the man protested modestly. "But it's better to check than to wonder." He secretly believed he had hit something, something everyone else had overlooked. Bill could sense it from his manner. But it really did pay to be thorough. They agreed on that. And they'd be checking much wilder ideas than that soon, if nothing else developed.

The agent walked over to the map and began to look for likely landing places. Artie was getting more slips from radio contact with his road vehicles. And Bill picked up a piece of paper, doodling in a serious way he liked to when he just wanted to think.

The FBI man came back from the map. "Did I hear that one of your people had a theory that they might be mountain climbers?"

"Oh, Diane," he remembered.

"Diane? I thought it was a ranger."

"Yeah. She's very much a ranger," he replied with a smile, not insisting on too much.

"Could I talk to her?"

"I'm afraid she's off today. She's probably out climbing herself, if I know her."

"Off? I thought you had all your men on today?"

Bill shrugged. "I didn't see any point. Besides, last night I thought this would all be over by now. She'll do her shift when she comes back. You can talk to her then." After a second he picked up his pad, to show that he was busy, calculating even, and the man went back to the map.

Maybe it was all that coffee. Or the man's repeated questions when he was beginning to get tired. But he was becoming irritated. That was when he realized the dog had been whining more constantly in the background. It had become an unconscious nagging that he meant to get to but his attention had been otherwise occupied. Like the need to piss when your mind's too busy, or the bed's too comfortable, or the dream too engrossing. And he suddenly realized how tiring it was to keep ignoring that sound. "Shut that dog up, somebody," he called out. And then, more reasonably, "Maybe it needs to piss. Take him for a walk, will you?"

A ranger returned from the radio room. "Any sign of Williams yet?" he asked plaintively.

"He drove into Jackson," someone replied. "Take one of the other cars." There were several keys on the board now. The man took one and went out.

Bill Shaw sat there, doodling. All of a sudden he looked up and called, "Hey, what was the description of that car again? Do you have it? Bring it here!"

Outside the air was still cold and damp, but the light was gaining strength, and behind the dense ground fog, which had yet to burn off, the sun was already up. "Easy, boy." The ranger took a turn of the leash around his hand as the dog began to pull, wanting to be extra careful that it didn't take off. They were behind the building, away from the road, walking across the parking lot toward the grass and bushes at the edge. There was frost and a light film of snow on the black tar surface. The dog, instead of seeming relieved at being out, was whining and pulling him back toward the rear of the building. Toward the few ranger wagons now parked there. Toward the only wagon which had a light accumulation of snow on the windshield and roof. Toward the only vehicle which wasn't joined to tire tracks of shiny black macadam which had been pressed through the frost during the night. The only wagon with the red-top just a touch off center.

"Not there. Not on our nice clean lot," the man chided the dog. He used his greater strength to pull the large animal across the slippery surface toward the side. "We can't have you making a mess in our parking lot, now can we?" he asked the dog.

Monday 7:30 A.M.

Teton campground was the only developed forest service campground which gave easy access to the Tetons from the Idaho side of the mountains. Norman crossed Teton Pass in the early morning dark, heading west, and turned north to Driggs, Idaho. From there he took the gravel road back east to Alta, Wyoming, and then turned into the "unimproved" road which continued up the canyon seven more miles to the campground.

It had been a slow trip, not just because he felt a need for caution as he swung through the dark mountain curves. There was also the roadblock and the traffic. The traffic was one of those little pluses, a surprise bonus that showed you that not everything in the world was against you. It was good news. In the middle of the night vehicles which had rushed out weeks before to pack the parks were now rushing out to beat the rush home. Everything would have been all right probably, but the crowd around him made Norman just that much more comfortable as he passed through the roadblock. He was held in a creeping line for ten minutes and then through a zigzag barrier at a crawl, stopped for only an instant as a deputy peered into the van (curtains all drawn back, noth-

171

ing to hide), and then waved impatiently on. (Keep it moving, please, traffic is backing up.)

There was a station wagon pulled off to one side. A solitary woman was standing there, tired and resigned, as she answered a deputy's questions, her bleached blond hair unusually bright in the floodlights and headlights. And then, slightly blinded but relieved, Norman was into the dark of the mountain road again. The surface was beginning to get slippery but the accumulation was not yet heavy. It did continue to snow, however.

It continued to snow until sometime after he had finally entered the campgrounds, sifting finer and finer until he could no longer tell if it was still coming down or being dusted off the trees by the wind. He found a parking place near the trail head, plainly visible to anyone coming out of the mountains. The women would be cold and tired after crossing, he felt. No picnics, no flowers. He didn't want them to walk right by him. And as for anyone else . . . It was too late to worry about that now. If anyone were looking for him, there, at that late date, then it would be over with as soon as possible. If anyone was looking for him, there, then it was all over already.

It was still quite early. As he settled in to wait he thought how different this now felt from the beginning of it all, coming over from Castro Valley to meet them at the Meat Market late in the evening, to sit and scheme outrageously over strong coffee that made them excited and talkative. He had tried to keep his voice below the background cover of the music because they were sitting around, actually planning a crime in public, over cheesecake. It was just that at first, the outra-

geousness he felt, the giddiness of his first con-
spiracy, a secret they almost consciously dangled
in front of others by meeting in public.

And then there was the intellectual challenge:
how to do it? And so they had accumulated detail,
and diagrams, and piles of (legal-size) yellow
paper which they left lying around with a casual-
ness that denied they could be serious. And because they weren't serious it was all right to continue. But Ruth was serious, he now realized, right
from the start, insuring that they all tended inevitably to the real act. Until she finally said, "Okay.
They have Dodge station wagons, sage green. We
need a wagon like it. You're the one who'll have to
get it," it had sounded reasonable. Exciting. More
of the game.

And now he finally saw that fantasy could be a
real, palpable form of energy, a Tinkertoy out of
which one could construct the future. For under
every move he now made he could sense those
easy daydreams, calcified, hardened by now into
the bones which supported this whole pattern.

And now anything could happen. Anyone could
come to get him, from in front or behind, rangers,
sheriffs, the women, anybody. And what could he
do? Tell them he was a faerie and skip off into the
woods? Hide under a toadstool? He realized that
his place was there, his thing was to wait. There
was nothing for him but to sit and wait to see
what happened. He waited. . . .

Two figures came toward him from the woods
but he could tell, even at that distance, that they
were neutral, neither friend nor foe. An older
couple, bundled up against the weather, without

packs and walking in shoes rather than hiking boots. He planned for them as he waited.

"Howdy."

They waved back, the automatic, almost mandatory friendliness of people in the woods. "You folks live hereabouts, by any chance?" he asked. He had shifted automatically into "straight" drag, he realized, and wondered if his voice was too low.

"Oh, no. Just camping," the man replied. Norman looked surprised. They had no equipment. The man waved over to an Airstream trailer. It was unusual to see one of the huge aluminum beasts off by itself, separated from its herd. To Norman camping meant a tent, but he switched his frame of reference automatically to be accommodating.

"Me too," he gestured over his shoulder at the van. "What's it like out there? I thought I might take a little hike, but the snow kind of put me off."

"Well, we didn't go far." The man seemed to be in charge of dealing with strangers. His wife just stood and smiled in a general way that neither included nor excluded him. "It started to pile in drifts as we got a ways up, so we came back. We just like a little walk after breakfast," he explained. A well-regulated life, it sounded. "How about you?" the man challenged.

"I'm just up here for vacation," Norman answered.

"Uh-huh," the man said, looking around suspiciously. His wife's smile was still a polite wall. Norman was sorry he had started with them and now he wanted some way to finish it off that wouldn't leave him stuck in their minds as odd or noteworthy.

"Actually I just pulled into this place to get some sleep. Made it up in three days from San Diego, and I tell you, that's driving." He had been going to lie about the state. Ruth didn't have a front plate on the van and he had backed into the space, but if he lied and they somehow saw his California plate he would never be able to talk around that, he decided.

"I'm actually headed through Yellowstone and on to Cody, Montana. Pick up the wife and kids." The woman's smile had more contact in it now. Norman continued merrily, having finally found his way. "Staying with her folks. I'm using my vacation to pick 'em up and we'll all go back together. They had a real nice visit." The couple nodded approvingly. "Had a good couple of weeks. That's enough," he explained, softening his voice. "The kids always like to visit Grandma and Grandpa, and of course they get spoiled silly. But, you know, her folks are getting older, and as much as they like it, it's tiring for them." He relaxed. He could see by their faces he was out of the odd category of a single man camping by himself. Everyone was nodding warmly and sympathetically at everyone else by now, everything was all right. "You folks traveling?" he asked the obvious with interest.

"This is our life," the woman replied, finally finding the conversation to her liking. "We retired early, and now we go where the wind blows us."

"We're headed for a Wally Buyem rally in Phoenix," the man explained.

"Well, it's good to work, and it's better to stop," Norman said earnestly.

"Ain't it the truth," they agreed.

Everyone wished everyone else a good trip. Then they walked back to their trailer and Norman went back to the van. He sat down on the sill of the open side door, stretched, and then leaned back against one of the jambs, wriggling until he found himself a comfortable position. "Well," he announced to himself, just to make it formal even though he already knew, "now I just have to wait and see who comes."

Monday 7:45 A.M.

"Do you want to take a break?" Mike asked her as they finished the steep climb to Inspiration Point and stood at the entrance to Cascade Canyon.

She looked him over quickly. He was panting and flushed, but quite as healthy as a young elk. He'd be fine. "No thanks, I'm fine," she answered, purposely misunderstanding him. A whole summer had passed but there was still a lot he hadn't caught on to yet. If he wanted to stop he would just have to say that. And admit he was winded.

And this was hardly the day for chickenshit chivalry. Suddenly she had no more patience. Mike went ahead, superficially leading. But she had almost complete control of their pace. All she had to do was step heavily near his heel and he scurried a bit faster. And she was pushing, herding him along the trail at the speed she wanted.

Why? she wondered. Hurry for what? Because she needed to, dammit! This was for her. Because she needed to know, if there were any way she could. And even if she couldn't find out a thing, she still needed to do it. Just to show respect for herself, for her own ideas and feelings, when no one else did. And even if she was wrong. Even if she proved that she was wrong ... well, that would be better than having to wonder forever. It's no big deal to be wrong, she thought. It's being "nobody" that wears you down.

They were moving out strongly along the flat bottom of the canyon. This was her backyard, familiar almost beyond recognition, so when she suddenly broke through a clearing in her thoughts and really saw it, it looked strange. She had spent so many days walking this path back and forth, checking hikers for passes and giving trail information. She had finally worn the experience down, pale and smooth, so now it served as a background for her thinking. The rhythm of hiking massaged body and mind so they slowly relaxed their hoarding clutch.

So why was she hurrying? What was she looking for? Anything! That was the answer. Anything at all. She wanted some trace, some sign before even that possibility was gone forever. Before she was left with nothing to fill up that space but a sour wondering.

The women would be gone. Long away. They had the time and the shrewdness. They knew the men would be busy looking in all the traditional places. For the traditional people. Busy men, self-important, and therefore blind. She had to admire the women. For seeing all that, and having the nerve to use it.

Or was it like that at all? Wasn't she just a hostile, frustrated woman looking for fantasy heroes because she felt so blocked in her life? By the time she got back they might have been caught, all of them, drunk and stupid, trying to bluff their way through a roadblock and then dragged helpless and chagrined before reporters as a lesson to others. The image made her shudder, and she was amazed. What humiliated them humiliated her. How strange it had all become.

Well, what was she looking for? What would satisfy her? She had found it was better to have a clear image of what she wanted when she was seeking. An abandoned rifle by the side of the path? A few bills lying in the snow like grouse feathers after a fox has made its meal? A gloating note tacked to a tree at the foot of some final pass?

How about just some simple sets of ordinary footprints in the right place around the right time? She might well find nothing more conclusive than that. And be lucky to have even that much.

And what then? What would she do next? She could always use Mike as her witness. Drag him back and make him report it to them. "Here," she could say. "He's one of you, so maybe you'll believe him!" Triumphant. Bitter. It was standard daydream material. Daydreams were great for spite, revenge, psychic warfare. In real life she had found she regretted that behavior. It was more satisfying just to imagine it.

"Rope!"

The sound came tiny but precise, a cameo word, from the half-mile of sheer rock wall on her right. Symmetry Spire. A party must be climbing it, up early, but she couldn't make them out. They had nicknamed it "Cemetery Spire" a few years ago, when seven climbers were gravely injured there in a single season. Accessible. You could walk right up to it and climb. Even if you had no business being there.

Mike had heard it too, and was also looking for the climbers. He was being a good sport. Although part of it was just being docile, not knowing how to resist her and speak up for what he wanted. "Can we go rafting instead?" he had asked her the night before, almost pleading. "It'll be my last chance."

"It's too cold," she had answered him.

"We could borrow some wet suits. . . ."

"Not tomorrow." And that meant maybe never. Was he aware of any irony? Early that summer, when she bought the raft, she was one of the first women in the area with her own. And there weren't many people who would go with her. When Mike had told the men at work they were going down the lower canyon, the Hoback, they had razzed him until he lost confidence and wasn't sure he wanted to go. Now just the thought of the rapids —Washingmachine, Champagne, Lunchcounter— made his eyes bright.

She thought of the river, and of how change had accelerated in the past few years. There were more than twenty commercial companies each operating a fleet of rafts there, and business would continue growing. From some landings trips left every few minutes, several rafts at a time, all overflowing. On weekends in midsummer, traffic was sometimes just like on the big highways.

This is a cynic's job, Diane thought. Out here an optimist would die of a broken heart. As more and more population built greater and greater pressure against their little sanctuary it would have to be swamped. People asked regularly, "Why isn't there a road on the other side of the lake, so we can drive right up to the mountains?" The answer to that one was quite simple, she thought. The reason why there aren't roads all over this little paradise is so that when someone robs the lodge they will have to hike out, and so I'll be the only one to know.

Monday 11:56 A.M.

Ruth was just waking from another short nap. Each time she dropped off she woke feeling, not better, but less worse. She still didn't feel good but the discomfort was actually tolerable now. The sky was still overcast and gray. She couldn't see the sun but it seemed to be late in the morning, maybe even around noon already. They were behind schedule. Norman would be worried. She sent a brief mental telegram to him explaining the situation. Perhaps he would sense something. Under the circumstances it was the best she could do.

Alice hadn't noticed that her eyes were open. She had just gotten the tiny backpacking stove out and was setting it up on a piece of rock she had found and laid flat on the snow. Perhaps it was that activity which had woken her up. Ruth watched her pour a small amount of fuel into the hollow under the single burner. Then, using several matches, finally shielding one successfully from the wind with her hand, she lighted the fuel. She watched it intently as it burned, heating the brass fuel tank under it, pressurizing that little container. So, when the flames were just about to die out, she turned the valve and gas rushed out of the burner and caught fire from the dying flames under it. It took a certain amount of skill and concentration to make it work, and it was more awkward than usual because she had evidently misplaced the small key which opened the valve. Instead she used a fork as a wrench, pressing the tiny square post into the space between the fork tines. Alice scooped up a potful of snow and placed it on the hissing burner before she checked Ruth again and noticed she was awake.

"I'm making tea," she said. "Would you like some?" She sounded tired.

Ruth nodded. They just looked at each other for a moment. "I'm feeling better," Ruth said, wanting to reassure her.

A vibrating hum came to them, as diffuse as the light and just as directionless. They looked around, trying to penetrate the sky in all directions. It was almost certainly a light plane somewhere over the mountains, or perhaps as far away as the valley. The canyon acted like a giant speaking tube, bouncing the sound from wall to wall and funneling it to them, so that its source was completely disguised. Very likely a search plane.

"Someone's coming," Ruth said suddenly. She had been sitting up, peering around her, trying to locate that hungry metal mosquito which was seeking their blood. Looking around to consider how they could hide. And over Alice's shoulder, like two tiny marks closing a quotation that included her head, were the two figures.

Alice turned and they both studied the advancing specks. They were only two dark marks in a snowy valley, but their motion looked steady, even, and practiced. "Could they be going somewhere else?"

"No. They're already on the South Fork. The only turnoff is into that trail which dead-ends at the cliffs. They pretty much have to be coming up here."

"What about the plane?"

"The plane won't be able to tell anything. I don't think the plane's any problem, unless they signal it. They couldn't radio back to the valley from here, but they could reach the plane."

"You think they're working together?"

"I don't know." They looked at each other, feeling blood pressure rise, muscles in their legs suddenly fretful.

"Look," Alice insisted, "they're probably just campers."

"Right," Ruth agreed tensely, "just some people who are out for a hike."

"And that's all we are, too. Just keep thinking that. *Realize* it! We are just two friends out camping. Let's not blow it all now by doing something weird." They watched the people approach. They got a bit bigger but revealed nothing more about themselves. Just two medium-sized figures with packs who came steadily toward them. But steadily, in the mountains, was not a fast run or even a trot. It was a gradual change with a subtlety which quickly exhausted their patience.

"Do you think we could pack up and hike out before they got here?" Ruth asked.

"How strong are you feeling?"

"Not super, but I could walk." Even the thought forced a frown, however.

"Well, I think they could catch up to us, if they

wanted to. And if they were wondering about us, it would make them more suspicious. But they are just hikers, probably. There's no reason not to just sit here, get our rest, leave when we want to. It's just that we feel suspicious. There is no reason at all for us not to be here. And we look fine, just like regular campers. We just have to get into that state of mind."

"Right," Ruth agreed.

"It's just because we're tired. We're getting spooky."

"Right," Ruth agreed.

"Let's have some tea now, and relax."

"Right."

Alice turned off the flame and dropped a pinch of leaves into the pot. She stirred them once and then they went back to watching the figures approach.

They came more rapidly now, the near space being less condensed than the distance. They looked up once, clearly recognizing their fellow hikers with a single hand overhead before they put their heads down for the climb. It seemed to be a woman and a man, but with heavy clothing, and hairstyles being what they were, it was impossible to be sure.

"Is there anything around?" Ruth asked, more to herself. And they looked over their campsite, trying to see it with a fresh, suspicious eye. There was nothing which struck them as a giveaway.

"Hi, there," Alice called as they were approaching over the last forty feet. The fellowship of the woods. Even now she hated to be insincere about it. They only nodded this time, still intent on their ascent, saving breath and concentration. But they were within the boundaries of their camp now, their territory, and she sensed if she didn't welcome them there then they would automatically be unwelcome. And she didn't want that kind of atmosphere.

They veered from the trail proper and forked over to the campsite. It was a woman and a young man. They seemed to be outfitted as they had walked, solidly, in equipment which was well broken in. "How's it going?" the man asked pleasantly, leading the way to them. Alice stood up to greet them, perhaps feeling more of an advantage on her feet. Ruth still had her legs half under her sleeping bag and sat there.

He walked right to them and looked the campsite over. Something in his manner made them feel inspected and they just waited. "Looks like it might clear," he said, glancing overhead after he spoke.

"Whew, that climb always gets me," the woman said, coming up beside them.

"It got me," Ruth said, wagging her head. Diane looked at her and nodded sympathetically.

"Been here long?" she asked.

"Not very," Ruth answered. "We set out just a little after sunrise. Wanted to get an early start."

"So did we," Mike said. "I'm surprised we didn't see you on the trail." He looked down the slope behind them. Ruth followed his eyes. Even to her inexperienced scrutiny it was clear that there was only one recent trail in the snow, only two clear sets of footprints. The ones just made. Mike looked at her, puzzled, but said nothing. But it was the woman's silent, even gaze that rattled her.

"What time *did* we start?" Ruth turned to Alice.

"It was actually just before sunrise, I guess, not after."

"Well," he cleared his throat and went on officiously, "you know, you're in a wilderness area here, and while it certainly is rugged in one sense it's actually quite fragile also. Man can put an imprint on nature which is indelible, often without even realizing it. So, we ask people to pick their campsites carefully, away from the trail with all its traffic." He gestured at the nearby trail with the rehearsed movements of a bad actor. "And off the slopes, which are susceptible to erosion," and he pointed sweepingly down at their feet.

"I was sick. It was the best we could do by moonlight," Ruth cut in snappishly. And then felt her stomach sink at what she had said.

"Are you two rangers?" Alice asked innocently, mostly to warn Ruth.

"We're with the National Park Service," Mike agreed.

"It's our day off," Diane explained, almost as if correcting him.

Mike hadn't meant to challenge Ruth. It was merely his last chance to do his job, a little gesture to the mountains around them, as if they might overhear and appreciate it. He was surprised that he had evoked such an unpleasant reaction. "Well, have a nice hike," he finished lamely, and started to pull off.

"How far did you want to go?" Diane asked him.

"Just up to the crest, the park boundary," he said, pointing up a few hundred feet where the trail arched out of sight.

"Then why don't you go on and I'll wait for

you here. I can use a break. And there's nothing like being on top all alone."

He smiled happily at her, feeling redeemed from his former clumsiness. "I'll be back in just a few minutes," he reassured her. "It isn't far."

Diane slipped her pack off with a grunt of relief and squatted down, leaning against it. They all watched Mike walk off without comment. "Would you like some tea? The water is still hot," Alice finally offered. Diane nodded and accepted a tin cup of lukewarm liquid which had some soggy bits of leaf floating in it. She took several polite sips, peering into the cup as she did, feeling the women steadily watching her. She tried to become absorbed in the tea but she couldn't even taste it. Finally, with a slight sigh, she gave in to her feelings and stopped pretending. She placed the cup in the snow beside her, not caring that it would immediately cool. Then she lifted her head to face the women.

"It certainly is lovely here," Alice said after a minute. They all looked at the remark as it hung, a bit of milkweed fluff on the air, before it blew away without a trace.

"You weren't well?" Diane asked Ruth.

"A little mountain sickness. I'm okay now," Ruth answered.

"It usually comes from hurrying when you're new to the area," Diane said. "A few hours' rest helps a lot." She looked back at them as steadily as they at her. It wasn't a staring match as much as the absorbed study of something which is fascinating.

"What's it like to be a ranger when you're a woman?" Alice asked.

Diane made a wry face. "You must be reading my mind. I was just thinking how that, more than anything else, is responsible for my being here now." She certainly had their attention and she couldn't think of any way to go but straight ahead. They didn't have more than a few minutes to resolve this once and for all.

"There was a robbery last night." Neither of them moved. "The people who did it seem to have gotten away. At least no sign of them had turned up by early this morning. The area is sealed off. Anyone leaving was searched. So were the campsites. And the bushes. But mostly just the highways. Because the robbers were two women. And a third person who drove." They sat the way a rabbit sits when a hawk is overhead.

"I told my chief that I thought they went into the mountains. You see, I think I saw them briefly in the lobby. One had a rope burn on her back. And they made some joke about an ice ax. . . . And also, it's the only thing that makes sense." In her pauses they could hear the wind. It was a light, thin song with a chill to it.

"You see," she explained, "I don't think he could imagine them doing anything like that. Because they were women. And he didn't pay much attention to me. I think for the same reason."

"You came to see for yourself," Ruth said to her.

Diane nodded. They could hear the plane again. It didn't come as close this time, and again it went away.

"Would you help me get my pack?" Ruth asked almost sleepily, twisting around to point at it, just a few feet away. Everything had slowed down now, and there was a clarity, an easiness, in which anything could happen naturally, and later might be impossible to understand or explain.

Diane took the few steps and brushed off the light covering of last night's snow without a comment. Then she dragged the heavy pack over to where Ruth was sitting and knelt next to her, as she knew the woman wanted.

"Was the other one hurt?" Diane asked.

"What do you mean?"

"Weren't there three of you?"

Ruth looked into her face from quite close. Both faces were relaxed and tired now, more sad than anything else. Ruth unzipped the side pocket of her pack and slid her hand into the space. Diane made no move to stop her, to struggle with her. Alice looked horrified but frozen in place. She was so young. So sweet and young, Ruth realized, feeling old herself. The rifle action was there, still loaded, and her hand felt stiff and cold the minute she touched it, the metal drawing all the life from her flesh. But even so, even in that dead husk of metal, grasped in that stiff dead hand, there was a tiny vicious germ of heat, hidden and waiting. Ruth slid it partly out of the pack.

"Don't make me kill you," she said simply. As if it might have been anything.

Diane sat back on her haunches. She needed more space to breathe. Mike was stepping and sliding down the slope toward them. Was it that long already? And what was she to do now, now that she knew, now that she was satisfied?

"Boy, that was something!" Mike stormed enthusiastically into the silence. He was slapping his hands together, whether from cold or excitement it wasn't clear. "It's murder up there. . . . Ready to go?"

"Not quite yet, Mike. Sit down. Have some tea," she told him flatly.

"I'm afraid we're all out. I can make some more. It will only take a minute," Alice offered nervously.

Mike looked puzzled. He wanted to be going and didn't sit as she asked. He continued to swing his arms at his sides with an excess of energy.

"We didn't introduce ourselves. I'd very much like you to know who we are at this point. My name is Diane. And this is Mike. He's my nephew, my sister's only child."

"Aw, Diane," Mike protested.

She ignored him. "He's only nineteen years old. I talked him into coming out here. I helped him get the job. I even dragged him along on this hike." Now he protested no more. There was an urgency in her voice that even he could hear, and he stood there stiffly, suddenly afraid and not knowing why.

"He seems like a very nice boy," Alice said, casting her vote, looking at Ruth instead of him.

"Where are you going from here?" Ruth asked her.

"Why, we could go almost anywhere," Diane offered. "We could go on with you a ways and circle back from further on, or we could go back the way we came."

"How far is it this way, through the mountains to the Teton campgrounds?"

"Once you get over the pass it's pretty easy, basically all downhill, and not too steep. I'd say five or six hours at a medium-good pace."

"And how long would it take you to get back down this way, the way you came?"

"If we went slowly, about the same. If we hurried, a little less. We're acclimatized," she explained, scrupulously revealing her advantages.

"What will you do when you get back?" Ruth challenged her. She knew the question was futile but she was unable to resist it.

"Take a hot shower," Diane answered simply. "We could go along a ways with you if you'd rather."

Ruth sighed and pushed her pack away disgustedly. They hadn't been prepared for this, for pursuit, for confrontation. It was too much. It suddenly had the feeling of getting out of hand. "No, I can't see why. It all comes down to the same thing, eventually. Why just prolong it? I don't see that there's anything to be gained by dragging it out." She stood up and turned around, starting to gather up her sleeping bag and stuff it into its carrying sack.

"Then I think we'll be going, if you don't need any help," Diane said.

"No," Ruth replied ironically, "all we want is to be left alone and we'll be fine, thanks."

Diane pulled her pack on, nodded to Alice, and walked out of camp. Mike took one last look around. "Well, good-bye," he said to Alice. Ruth was busy with her pack. He followed his aunt across to the trail and started down toward the canyon.

Ruth busied herself with breaking camp, condensing and packing and checking for litter. After a minute of watching her pack Alice realized there was really nothing to talk about, and she too bent to that work. They had only made camp in a minor way, there was comparatively little to do. And even when they were packed Ruth didn't look at her. She had pulled into some guarded inner place where she could be alone and without distraction. She looked resigned.

"Might as well get on with it," she said, her eyes still turned away, and led the way upward toward the trail and the ridge.

"What else could we have done?" Alice asked.

"Nothing," Ruth said. "You didn't want me to shoot them, did you? And it seemed almost as strange to think of taking them as hostages. So I don't know." She shrugged. They picked up speed, trying to walk away from their thoughts as well as the place.

The descent from the pass was a steady lope. Mike and Diane yielded to the momentum demanded by gravity, stepping out to relieve the strain on their knees, the continuous controlled fall forward taking much less energy per mile than constantly braking and resisting. It was a bounding motion which suited her mood very well. Diane felt exultant. She was right. She had been right all along. No one had believed her and she had still been right. She hadn't believed herself, and she had still been right. She would never ignore that independent little voice again, she pledged, silently apologizing, as if to another person. God, she was glad she had climbed the mountain that morning!

Her head was a chaos of celebration. Several different voices, all hers, reminded her of things she had said which others had ignored, things she had seen and heard and come to doubt herself. Gloating voices experimented with clever remarks, devastating put-downs, and long triumphant speeches of a kind which would never be tolerated anywhere but on the stage. It was like being drunk, and like being drunk it was mixed with the worry that she had gone too far, was enjoying herself too much, was a bit out of control, and might throw up.

"What was that all about?" Mike asked after a few minutes, after the panting and stomping had evened out to a regular rhythm, after his muscles had warmed up again and he had his breath back. They were almost out of sight of the pass. The women had long since disappeared over the crest.

"What do you mean?" Diane asked.

"That weird scene at the top. What was going on?"

"Oh. When you left they were worried that you would cite them for illegal camping. They got pretty upset about it, actually. I think you frightened them. I told them it was just a warning and you were probably quite satisfied with having made your point, but . . . guilty consciences I guess. . . ."

"I never meant to come down that hard on them, you know. I just wanted to be sure they understood how easy it would be to scar up that slope."

"I don't think they're likely to do that again," she reassured him.

"Diane," he asked after a minute, "why did you offer to go with them?"

"One of the women wasn't feeling well. I thought they might need some help. But apparently they thought they could manage. . . ."

After a few minutes he dropped back a little further, giving her more freedom to swing her arms and body without bumping him. And more privacy. Apparently he was satisfied.

But Diane still had things to consider. On the mountain the women had had guns. They had even threatened her, although she hadn't felt it quite that way. She had reacted as if it were mostly a threat to Mike, or at least that she was responsible for him and had to protect him. Of course she could have gotten killed. But now they could no longer hurt her. She had no excuse for not reporting them. They had committed an armed robbery and stolen a large amount of money. It was her duty as a ranger, and as a citizen, to turn them in immediately. And she had already lied to her nephew, protecting them. . . .

How she looked forward to walking up to Bill Shaw's desk. He'd have his head down. Busy. Big man with important business. "I know where they are." No. Not the tone she wanted. "By the way, they're up past Cascade Canyon. Just like I told you." He would mumble, busy with his papers. Fine, if that's how he wanted it. She would just sit herself at a desk nearby, pick up a newspaper, and relax for a while. "What did you say?" he would suddenly ask. She would take her time putting the paper down. Finish the paragraph first, while he waited.

She ran his double take through her head several times, adjusting it like a movie director, checking with a critical eye for the most satisfying sequence. She wanted amazement, embarrassment, hurt pride, and rage either in rapid sequence or all on his face simultaneously. One time she had him leap to his feet, spilling coffee all over his desk but unable to take his stricken eyes from her face while the creamy brown blotch spread steadily through his papers.

And I don't even hate him, she thought at one point. Imagine if I hated him. . . . But she was very angry with him, with his treatment of her, and his complete blindness. Because he had no idea, she was sure, that she was so angry, or why. He wasn't a bad person. Not at all. He just needed a little lesson.

And the head movies always ended there, she realized. Right after the episode "When Bill Shaw Learns His Lesson." But the story didn't really end there. The women would be caught. If anyone in the capturing party had personally taken offense at their boldness they would be pushed and shoved and perhaps beaten to show them their punishment had already begun. And then they would disappear, except for a final newspaper item or two, behind stone and iron and silence, for years. It didn't seem a fair trade: their lives for a few minutes of her satisfaction. And she might not even get satisfaction. Shaw might let her down completely and not make any of the faces she had planned for him.

They hadn't hurt anyone. That wasn't exactly true. They had hit Allen on the head, but he didn't seem to blame them for it. They had done it only when he fought them. They had seemed quite concerned, he said. But they hadn't hurt *her*. They could have killed Mike and her. If they'd hid the bodies well no one would have found them until spring. It might have been very different if they were two men she had stumbled upon while they were fleeing. Very different. And in fact she suddenly realized she might never have attempted to follow them in the first place if they had been men.

But just where did that leave her? Grateful that she hadn't been killed? Wonderful. And what did she owe the others who hadn't killed her, all the thousands of people she knew who conceivably could have closed her account permanently and had not? Did she owe each of them infinite gratitude and exemption from the law? It wasn't right to let criminals go free, just because they were women. With the same rationale men could let all male criminals go. And another unpleasant thought intruded: how much did the women really matter at all, how much were they just pawns in her undeclared war with Bill Shaw?

But they were felons, clearly guilty of robbery and assault. It was intolerable that such people go free. If she went with her feelings and anyone ever found out, she would be dismissed for sure. And she might face criminal charges as well. Her pride trapped her, she now saw, and she wished she didn't have the power to turn all of this around. For it was all so obvious now, what they were doing and where the third of their party was.

Once you knew they were climbing, you knew they were heading for Teton campground, on the other side. And once you knew that, you knew someone was certainly meeting them, had to be meeting them there. For without that they would be stranded and obvious and vulnerable. Once you had penetrated the first subtle barrier of subterfuge you had them. Like snails they were, with only one thin shell around them, and that shell only as thick as an idea, an attitude. No protection at all from the stomping of a heavy boot, she thought sadly. Why was this so hard? She had always thought that decisions about right and wrong should be things you could feel, choices you made naturally. Well, fortunately there was still time. Time to work on her feelings, to bring her emotions in line with her duty. Because, in the last hard analysis, she knew what was really right.

Monday 12:40 P.M.

It couldn't have been more than twenty minutes since they left the women, which meant that the women, hiking in the opposite direction, were about forty minutes away. Mike and Diane had just rotated places, Mike going ahead and Diane falling behind him. There was a different feeling to be ahead or behind on the trail. In front there were constant small decisions about where on the trail to walk, where the footing was the most secure or comfortable. And the person ahead was more likely to see the wildlife before it flushed and darted. It was more interesting, and more tiring. Behind, it was possible to just follow, sucked along in the wake of another consciousness, freeing one's own for whatever. After a mile or two the difference could easily be felt. They changed places regularly to share both experiences, and for some variety which made the distance go faster.

They were following the trail in a long arc around a smooth stone hump to their left, a small, open meadow to the right, a bit swampy up to the pines on the other side, when Mike saw two rangers in uniform hurrying toward them. It seemed unlikely but even at several hundred yards it looked like Chuck and The Shadow, the two who had been working the lobby with Bill the night before. And as they came closer they could be seen (even more unlikely) to be wearing sidearms in holsters on their belts. Mike looked back once to see if she had noticed.

Diane had noticed. Ryner was in the lead and his bulk was unmistakable to her even at that distance. Huge and lumbering, he charged up the trail, snowplowing, not bothering to lift his feet above the snow surface. Chuck, looking like a slender, blond stork leashed to a great bear, struggled to keep up. She had never seen them armed before.

"Hey," Mike called as they came closer, "what are you guys doing up here?"

The men continued uphill toward them, slightly winded, not answering yet. Mike automatically stepped off the trail to make room for Ryner, who ignored him and acknowledged Diane with only a nod.

"We're chasing bandidos, my friend," Chuck said.

"Really?"

"Well, sort of," he admitted. "We finally cracked this one. Bill figured they came through here last night. With any luck they're out the other side and the sheriff has already grabbed them."

"The sheriff?"

"Yeah. Bill had him come in to Teton campground and wait for them to show. This is just a routine trail sweep. We've got to check that they didn't ditch the money along here. Or try to double back or hide along the way," he added as an afterthought.

Diane was afraid to say anything. She hadn't

expected this. There were still several hours separating her from Bill Shaw, and she was unprepared.

"How did you figure all that?" Mike asked, properly impressed.

"We found the car. And their disguises were in a trash barrel. Wigs, dresses, and all. Pretty clever, if you think about it. It was three men, all made up, who ditched their stuff and hiked out through here. You haven't seen three men ripping through here, have you?"

"No," said Diane quickly.

"We saw only two women," Mike explained, "and one of them was sick."

Ryner turned, interested for the first time. "Which way?" he demanded.

"Right through the pass."

"We'll check 'em out. Let's get going. I want to run them down before they screw up the trail."

"They were camped illegally," Mike said. "Just below Hurricane Pass. I almost cited them, but I decided that a good warning would be enough for the first time." He was immediately sorry he had said it. Ryner looked at him expressionlessly before he turned to go.

"I'll go along with you," Mike offered. "There's only two of you and three of them. You can use all the help you can get."

"You're not armed," Ryner cut him off. "You'd be in the way."

"You're no longer on duty." Diane struggled to keep her voice even.

"I'll stay back," Mike promised. "I'll just be there for backup, in case one of you gets winged or something." The thought of being shot had never occurred to Chuck and his eyes went briefly out of focus as he considered it.

"You never know. Something might happen and I could go for help, if you needed it," he went on, selling himself as an assistant, trying to let them know he didn't want to hog it, and suddenly desperate to see, to be there.

"Your parents are expecting you on an early plane tomorrow," Diane argued.

"I can get a later one."

"I'm responsible for your safety, and you're going back just as I promised."

"Aw, Diane!"

"After you're home you can do anything you want." She was fortunate she could still manipulate him. He *had* to be kept away from those two women. She saw his shoulders slump in defeat and felt greatly relieved.

"Maybe you could go on over to White Grass Station," Chuck sympathized, hating to see him so embarrassed. "They could probably use some help there. They're waiting in case they drop into Death Canyon from Alaska Basin and try to double back into the park."

"They would never head down Death Canyon in a light snow," Mike said sullenly, looking at the ground and unable to meet anyone's eye. "It's too dangerous."

"C'mon!" Ryner cut in. "We're wasting time."

"I'll see you back at the dorm," Chuck called as he automatically trailed Ryner up the bleak slope.

Diane watched them go with mixed feelings. Mike was out of it. But for the women, she felt a chill. Well, her decision was made, and "naturally." Her mouth had refused to betray them to

Ryner. She hadn't made a decision, she was the decision.

Even if she had never heard about the elk, she wouldn't have trusted Ryner. But that made it definite. It crystallized something she had felt about him all along. God help those women, she thought with a sigh of resignation, and turned to lead her sullen nephew back toward civilization.

"I don't care how much it costs," the woman said,
"I don't think there's nuthin' that'll replace cof-
fee." She lifted her insulated cup in salute and
Norman tipped his politely back.

They were a pleasant family. A carved wood
plaque on the back of their camper said they were
"The Bakers." Carol worked over in Afton sewing
down jackets and vests. Her husband was a car-
penter. Their two young children sat nearby, peace-
fully sharing a small hole in the ground which
they were both poking with sticks.

In the midmorning they had pulled in alongside
of Norman and promptly unloaded children, folding garden furniture, and a card table and sat
down over fresh coffee to play cribbage. Within a
short time Norman was seated with them, coffee
in hand, passing the day. Norman was glad for
their friendliness, and also he felt much less conspicuous than if he had been sitting alone, a single
man just waiting in a campground with nothing to
do.

"They don't appreciate craftsmanship," she complained, holding up her fingers.

Behind her head the sheriff's car pulled into the
clearing and swung across the road, blocking it, in

a sudden gravel-crunching arc. The sheriff and a deputy stepped out immediately, sweeping the area with their eyes, radar-like, back and forth, as they walked around the car and stood together. There they could talk in low voices and still both face the campers. Everyone stopped and looked up.

"They certainly look all business," Carol commented, her head turned almost completely away from him. She didn't seem to expect replies much of the time. Her husband was a quiet man.

Norman felt his hand begin to shake. He set his coffee down immediately. The tremor passed as soon as he let go of the cup. His leg muscles bunched for a run to the driver's seat of the van. He measured the space between the police car and the woods to see if the van could squeeze around the blockade. He imagined them shooting as they followed. He could never get away. Not from that powerful car and the guns. The men trained to capture.

"I used to sew an entire garment myself," she said, turning back to him when nothing seemed to be happening at the sheriff's car.

I could walk around the van and slip into the woods, Norman thought. If they didn't see me it might be a while before they realized I was gone.

"When I was done I would sew in a label that said, 'This Garment was Handcrafted by Carol.'"

I could stay parallel to the road until I got to a town. How far is it to Alta?

"You can bet that every one of those was as perfect as I could make it. I couldn't say it was just a job, you know? It may sound silly to you, but I couldn't be detached when it had my name on it."

Alta is too small. I'd be completely obvious there.

Driggs. I'd have to get all the way to Driggs. Damn! That's a hell of a walk.

The sheriff was gesturing with his right arm, slicing the campground into sections, pointing to a central spot in the gravel loop which ran around to each campsite, and then back to the car which blocked the exit.

"Now they want to go to piecework. An assembly line," she sneered, genuinely insulted. "They say it will be faster. And they're going to lower the rate, too, because of that. All they'll get is fast, shoddy work." She spread her hands. It was so obvious, her gesture said, you had to wonder how the world could go so wrong when it was all so easy to see.

There must be some vacation houses around. I could probably break into something. Spend the night. Maybe a few days, if I don't get too hungry.

"This must be a bore to you."

"Not at all," Norman assured her quickly, focusing directly on her face again. "I think a lot about the same kind of things myself, in my own way. I was distracted a bit by the sheriff, though. I wonder what he wants here? Looks sinister to me."

She turned back to look again. It had occurred to Norman that since they hadn't rushed over and arrested him they couldn't know exactly who he was. He had assumed that the women were caught and forced somehow to confess. That they realized he would be caught sooner or later anyway and it might be easier and safer for him if he were just picked up before he got himself hurt. They certainly knew he had no interest whatsoever in being hurt.

"I think I'll just wander over and see what's up. Save my place"—he pointed down at his chair, managing a smile—"I'll be right back." He kept her coffee mug in his hand. It looked much more casual and friendly. And there was no mistaking it for a gun, either. If they did somehow recognize him they could take him quietly with no fuss or damage. That would definitely be best, if it had to come to that. He'd have to ask if he could return the cup, he reminded himself. She was a nice woman. It wouldn't do to walk off with her cup. He was willing to walk off with over a hundred thousand dollars, of course. Well, you had to draw the line somewhere, he decided.

They had split up. The deputy had gone to the center spot the sheriff had indicated, where he could watch the entire campground. And the sheriff was starting over to the first campsite. Norman headed for the deputy, cup firmly in hand. As he went, several other campers saw him and started along with him, eager to know also. A small, loose pack gathered and headed over.

The deputy waved them off. "Please return to your campsites and stay there. We'll be by to talk to you in a minute. Please return to your campsites and stay there. The sheriff will come by to talk to you in a minute," he repeated twice, sounding like a military PA announcement.

The campers turned, chagrined by being ordered about in public. Norman was relieved a bit. He had nothing on him that was incriminating. They didn't seem to have a good description of him or the van. He might be able to slip away later. Or . . . who knows?

"They don't have to be like that," she sympathized when he came back. "Would you like some more coffee?"

It took the sheriff about ten minutes to work his way around. "This your camper?" he asked Norman in clipped, official tones. Norman was sitting closest to him.

"I'm over there," and he indicated the van.

"When did you arrive?"

"Last night."

"Where are you coming from and where are you going?"

"I came from San Francisco. I think I might just wander on over to Teton and Yellowstone next. They should be nice and quiet, after the weekend. Do you know if there's any campsites available?"

"Couldn't say. Have you seen three men come down that trail while you've been here, or have you seen three men leave this campground at any time?"

"The only people I've seen leave have been an older couple in an Airstream."

The sheriff looked him over for a minute and then moved on with just a polite nod to Carol.

Monday 2:05 P.M.

"I'm sitting for a minute," Chuck called, and that was all. He brushed the snow off a rock and sat. He didn't look up to see if he was heard; he didn't peer after Ryner to see what his reaction would be.

He had been waiting for a break for almost half an hour now. But Ryner was in no mood. He had pushed, keeping up a demanding, gradually aggravating pace, with no indication that he intended to stop in the near future. Ever since they left Mike and Diane. He led as if he smelled his quarry, hurrying more than Chuck thought was reasonable. And making the implicit demand that he keep up.

Now without looking he could see from the fading edge of his vision that Ryner had backtracked. He was returning to be nearer to Chuck, to be close enough to influence, to throw the shadow of his personality onto him and make him obey. That was why Chuck started fussing with his boot. Any reasonable person would have taken a break. He was getting tired and there was no sense in killing themselves.

Ryner shuffled back toward him along the snowy trail, impatient to be noticed, to get them moving again. Chuck concentrated on his laces. He tightened them quickly, hurrying in spite of himself, angry that he was letting himself be cowed. He was done and it was still too soon. Ryner was standing over him, arms folded across his chest, staring stonily down.

Chuck examined the sole of his hiking boot. Caught in the black Vibram which was cleated like a snow tire was a small pebble. He took his jackknife from his pocket and used the screwdriver to lever the stone out. He hadn't felt it but it could conceivably make his foot sore at that spot in time. Or make his cleats slip when he was climbing on rock. It was sensible enough, but it was mainly a way of resisting the unpleasant pressure he felt from Ryner.

"You'll rest when we've done our job," came from high above those huge boots. Without looking up Chuck got wearily to his feet and followed.

It was stupid to be charging along like this. There were only two women ahead, Chuck thought angrily. The robbers were long gone. Unless, of course, they were caught in the storm and had to wait it out. Unless they threw up a quick bivouac under some protected ledge . . . They had passed just such a campsite, right where Mike said it would be. And the depth of the impressions in the snow placed them there at about the right time. And afterward there had been only that double set of prints and nothing else in all that snowy wilderness. It didn't explain what had happened to the third of their group. Or why they appeared to be women. But even after these quibbles the tracks were clear, solitary, and had a terrible potential. Chuck had no wish to overtake them. He cursed the snowstorm that might have held them back.

Almost as if reading his thoughts, Ryner assured him over his shoulder, "Don't worry, we'll get them before they reach the sheriff." And then as an afterthought, "I've been waiting for something like this. C'mon, this is going to do us a lot of good."

The afternoon was overcast, cold and a bit dismal. After a time the Bakers' little girl lost interest in the dirt and began to poke her smaller brother with the stick. Carol and her husband put them to sleep in the front of the camper. Norman caught a single wink pass from her husband to her and a minute later she announced that they would probably take a little nap too. That sly devil, Norman thought, turning in his mug and going back to his van. The Bakers bundled into the camper with enthusiasm, pulling the door shut behind them.

After the round of questioning, the sheriff had the deputy pull their car from its blockading position to the opposite end of the campground, past Norman, to just before the start of the trail. They backed behind a clump of high bushes where it would be concealed at first from anyone entering the grounds from that side. Then they varied the wait by alternately standing outside until their feet got cold and sitting in the car with the motor on and the heater, until they got warm again. After a while someone who apparently had some slight acquaintance with the sheriff walked over tentatively. No one waved him away and Norman and a few others moved close enough to hear.

"Say, what's going on, Artie?" the man asked.

"It's the lodge robbery. They expect those people to come through here." He had his arms folded across his chest, leaning back against the fender of the car. "But I don't know. That was the last we heard. We can't get any radio transmission here in this canyon. They should have been through by now, unless something happened to them. There are some rangers coming in from the other side to check the trail and flush 'em if they're still in there. Pick up the pieces if they got themselves hurt or froze."

"They got them trapped up there?"

"They think it's three men is all I know. We'll stop anybody who comes out and check 'em over good, just to make sure. Nobody gets out of there without our knowing that they're okay."

It took Norman only a minute to make up his mind. He couldn't stand the idea of sitting there until the women were grabbed, unsuspecting, perhaps even as they were running toward him. If only they could bury the money. Or even burn it. But with their packs full of stolen bills there was no way they could get out.

He pulled his coat tighter around him and started up the trail, past the police car.

"Where the hell do you think you're going?"

"I just want to take a little hike before dinner. Work up an appetite. Before it gets dark."

"You can't go up there. There are dangerous criminals up there. What if they decided they needed a hostage and put a gun in your ear? You wouldn't like that, now would you? Please go back to your campsite and stay away from this end. And that goes for the rest of you, too. If there's going to be any trouble we don't want anybody down this end. Got that?" Everyone moved off, slowly, but not so disgruntled now that they had their explanation. Besides, it continued to get colder and dimmer and waiting outside was hard work for those who were paid to do it, not a casual amusement for bored campers.

Norman climbed into the van and sat on the floor. He slipped his pocketknife out of his jeans and started to clean his fingernails. There was nothing else to do. He had a habit for waiting, an idea he liked to hold in his mind like a mental sour ball.

He wanted his own home in San Francisco. A place to plant some flowers and vegetables. On sunny days he pictured having breakfast on a small deck overlooking the city. Or bringing out a drink in the evening. A place to be alone or with company. When he thought about it, it had always been peaceful and satisfying, but now he wondered, was this all worth it?

While he had continued to save earnestly, prices had gone on rising. During those last few years when he optimistically thought he was moving toward his goal he had actually been falling back further and further from it. Until he finally realized that working on salary he could never catch up. That was why this idea of Ruth's, coming, when it did, had seemed like such a miracle then. Now, alone in the cold and fading light, it seemed not at all worth it.

Monday 2:52 P.M.

The women faced a succession of ridges, long waves of rounded stone washing through this part of the basin. The smooth and high places were windswept and clean. In troughs and irregularities the snow collected, a few inches here, a few feet there. Their march was across them now, constantly up and down. The overcast had continued to thin out but had not broken. There was no true sky, no blue and penetrable space available to them yet. It was like granite overhead, reflecting the gray stone beneath and around them.

Alice checked Ruth, measuring her movements for a few steps, and was satisfied. She was striding more easily and rhythmically than before. "How're you feeling?" she called out.

"Better. My headache's gone."

"We're getting used to the altitude. How's your stomach?"

"Well, I still have one."

"Would you like to stop and rest?"

"Why don't we just slow down a little?" They relaxed into an easy walk and Alice stretched her arms out and back to ease the weight on her shoulders.

Ruth shifted the load on her back too. "Why don't we dump some of this stuff?"

"What?"

"Let's drop everything but the money. We could dig a hole and bury it."

"Out here?"

Ruth realized Alice had stopped cold.

"You're kidding!" Alice said in the same tone.

"Not the money, the extra stuff. The extra weight."

"We can't leave that here."

"Sure we can. We were careful. They can't trace anything."

"That's not the point. We have no right to harm this place. We can't turn this into a garbage dump." Alice plucked her glasses and rubbed the good lens with her mitten as if that might clarify something.

"How can that matter now?" Ruth countered stiffly.

Alice squinted back belligerently. But with her glasses on she relaxed again. "Look, I understand how you feel. Anything you don't want, just give it to me and I'll carry it out."

Ruth knew Alice and she knew they had reached the bottom line. "No," she said after a minute, "it's okay."

"Really. I don't mind."

"No, you're carrying more than me already. As long as we're standing here anyway, why don't we sit down and take that break?"

Ruth selected a mound of stone shaped like half a huge watermelon rising from the snow. They scrambled up the sloping side and perched on the hump, letting their legs dangle comfortably over the curve. Alice took a bag of trail munchies from her parka pocket and pushed them toward Ruth.

"We couldn't bury anything anyway. It's all rock," Alice said, starting to chew her gorp. She took the liter plastic bottle she had been carrying under her parka and shook in a pack of Wylers. Fifteen minutes before she had filled the container with snow and let it melt from her body heat.

"You're probably right." Ruth looked down at the bag of nuts and dried fruit with distaste.

"Eat something," Alice encouraged.

"My stomach doesn't want it."

"Your stomach doesn't know how much trouble you can get into. At this altitude, to stay healthy, you can need up to five quarts of water and five thousand calories a day. That's like two hundred fifty packs of Life Savers. And at the same time you could lose your appetite."

"When I used to diet I wouldn't eat that much in a week." After a minute she noticed, "My butt's getting cold. Why don't we eat while we walk. We can take our time. . . ."

They grunted to their feet, stamped their boots to get the blood moving, and skittered down the rock to the trail. Both of them felt better. It was getting later and later, but that worry was offset by the fresh surge of energy flowing through them. At the next rise Alice continued, as she had for several miles, to pivot for a moment and look out as far as she could in all directions. Particularly down the trail behind them. This time, for the first time, she saw something.

There were two spots on the trail, moving spots, heading in their direction with what seemed like a strong forward momentum. They were a good bit behind still. And then, as she followed Ruth down into the next hollow, they were gone again, cut off from seeing each other by the distance and the snow and the stone.

"There's someone behind us," she said reluctantly, as they topped the next rise and she saw they were closer.

"Can you tell anything?" Ruth asked, staring at the furiously striding figures.

"I can make out ranger uniforms," she said. "And hats. I don't think there's any mistake."

"What do you think they're doing here, coming this way?"

"Probably just some trail work."

"I thought we were out of the park by now. More than half an hour ago."

"Right. We are. I just don't know. But it shouldn't be anything too serious. If we just keep on, mind our business, and remember that we're just a couple of innocent hikers."

"We have nothing to worry about as long as we don't do anything foolish," Ruth echoed. "We probably look perfectly normal to them. Not a bit suspicious; just don't panic."

"Right," Alice agreed with her, still looking back at the approaching movement.

That was when they heard the shot.

"What did you do that for?" Chuck spun around and clapped his hand to his ear.

"You're a big boy. You know what's going on." Ryner was still peering intently into the distance.

Chuck's ear was ringing and felt a little deaf. "You don't know who those people are! You want to shoot them, and you don't even know who they are. . . ."

"I wasn't trying to shoot them," Ryner contradicted coldly. "It's too far. That was a warning shot. You saw me shoot up in the air."

Chuck felt his outrage dissolve as he watched his partner, the heat washed away by a flush of clammy, kidney-twitching cold. And suddenly this felt like no place to argue. Like once in a strange bar a drunk had turned to him and taken a switchblade from his pocket, snapping it open with a jab from a dirty thumbnail. "This mother's so sharp I could cut your liver out before you even felt it go in," the man had promised. Like that. Another time when it felt wrong to stick up for what he believed in.

"They didn't stop, did they? They just popped over that ridge like a couple of lousy woodchucks going for their holes."

Chuck was still staring at him.

"While you're bullshitting they're getting away."

"They're not getting away. They've got no chance against us, up here."

"This is where they find that out," Ryner agreed. And he pointed.

Ryner still held his gun. He pointed with it, gestured, like he had forgotten he held it, or like something familiar he enjoyed in his grip. And every time he waved it by Chuck, crossed his belly, Chuck winced, felt his body tighten and brace against it, revealing part of a fear he wanted very much to keep secret, until finally, against his will, wanting least of all, less than anything in the world, to call attention to the gun, he could not help staring down at it.

So when Ryner flicked the barrel toward the trail, looking at him significantly, Chuck moved out at once. He went quickly as he had been told.

"Keep low. Remember they have rifles." And Ryner added, "Now we're going to run them until they drop. Then they'll be easy."

When she heard the shot Ruth charged over the ridge, missing the narrow path, and found herself wading frantically through waist-deep powder. "Are they shooting at us?" she gasped.

"Get back on the trail," Alice answered, also running. "They can't see us now. Come back over here or you'll wear yourself out."

"They could have been shooting at someone else." Ruth was struggling now to lift her feet high enough to clear the deep snow, heading over to Alice.

"Sure."

"But nobody else is here, right?"

"Right. I don't think so."

"We've got to get out of here!" And she scrambled onto the trail next to Alice, bumping into her in haste, and then immediately pushing past and starting down the path again.

Alice followed right after, wanting to be calm, wanting to stop and think reasonably about what to do next, and totally unable to stand still while Ruth was frantically running ahead of her. They were moving sloppily, kicking snow as they went, stumbling and squandering their energy, too charged up to talk, running out their panic.

It was only a minute before they were drenched with sweat and gasping for air. They continued moving because it was intolerable to stay still now.

They struggled up the next rise and once over the top, hidden by yet another mass of earth, they sucked at the air for a moment together, leaning on their ice axes.

"They can catch us. I don't think we can do it. . . ." They stood there, panting and looking at each other. "I'm sorry. I can't do this much longer. I'm sorry, Alice."

"Don't feel bad, hon. I don't think it would help even if you could."

They looked back. They could see little but the snowy hill that sheltered them for the moment. Turning forward they could see the trail starting down, still rising and falling, but each time ending a bit lower. They were nearing the end of the basin. Soon there would be the drop-off and the way would descend more sharply into an almost flat, narrow valley, walled by steep cliffs on both sides, the trail going straight down the middle, exposed for several miles, before diving into the last growth of woods which surrounded the campground.

"How long before they catch up?" At that thought they both began hiking again, starting off together and staying close for comfort and contact.

"I'd guess less than half an hour. They're not loaded down like we are."

"And how long to the campground?"

"Two hours. A little more, maybe."

"What if we leave the packs?" Ruth finally asked, hating to say it again.

"I'm afraid it's too late for that."

"Not to hide them. If we left them by the trail where they would see them. If they picked up the packs it might be enough to slow them down. And we could go faster. We could scatter the money around. And they'd have to stop to pick it up."

"We couldn't be sure. They'll know what we're up to."

They pushed on. They didn't know what else to do. This was a part of the robbery they had never imagined, never planned for. It was supposed to be a quick hike out. Not a hunt.

Figuring and refiguring. Half an hour behind. Two hours to go. It never came out right no matter how many times she calculated, but Ruth still did not want to accept the answer. She heard her feet pressing through the fresh snow, crushing it down as they cut across the smooth and trackless hollows. It made her look back. And she saw they had laid down their path like a giant line of fuse. They were the explosives attached to one end of it. And the rangers were like the spark, moving rapidly up. She realized they were hurrying hopelessly away from a giant explosion.

Ruth thought about Posey. This was the longest she had been away since she was born. And now . . . She tried to be realistic, to imagine what it would be like if she were captured and jailed, for years. Would they do that to the mother of a young child? Sure. And if she were killed?

She remembered the letter. For the first time, she realized how naïvely she had written it. She hadn't, she now realized, believed a word of it. She felt it was the right thing to do. But she hadn't really expected to die. Not at all. Or even be caught. Or she never would have tried it. She had been kidding herself. It was a game that had soured, and gone real.

The thought reminded her of Posey and the

games they had played, the hiding, teasing, and fooling. What an incredibly sweet child, she thought, in a sudden rush of uncontrolled feeling.

"We have to think about surrendering," Alice cut into her remembering. Ruth looked at her, still considering something that had occurred to her.

"We have to be realistic," Alice went on. "I want us to get out of this without being hurt. And at the very least, I want us to be alive. . . . It looks pretty hopeless to me. No place we could hide for long. And that wouldn't even help. I don't like them shooting at us. I don't trust them. . . . What do you think?"

"Do you think we could fool them somehow?"

"What?"

"Well, look at those tracks. . . ." Ruth pointed back at the line in the snow which ended at their heels. "It's such a perfect giveaway that it seems like we don't have a chance. But if we could make it go somewhere, they would probably follow it. That's what they're doing right now. If only we could make a path somehow, and not be at the end of it. All we need is a little time."

Alice chewed her lip and studied the trail.

"If we go over there," Ruth pointed at Battleship Mountain rising gray off to their right, "and come back by a different route, and brush off our tracks with branches, they may think we're still hiding up in the rocks."

Alice studied the distant mountain and then the trail, appraising it all. "That's an idea. . . . That mountain is too far off. They'd catch us going there. And you can't brush tracks out of deep snow. But we can do something, if we find the right place. Let me go ahead." And she charged off.

They ran down the next slope and started up again. It was getting toward the lower edge of the basin. The glaciers had scraped less deeply and efficiently here, their colossal housekeeping less complete. There were more outcroppings and irregular pieces of rock showing through the snow. Now they came toward two ridges shaped like a "V," which they approached from the bottom. On the left, paralleling the trail for several hundred yards, was a line of rock, large humps which appeared to rise from deep in the ground like surfacing whales, interspersed with smaller piles which seemed to have been dumped there. The trail ran alongside them but stayed on the flat smooth area at their base. Cutting across the trail at right angles was the next ridge, running off to the right for hundreds of yards. About forty yards out this ridge also rose from the snow and became solid rock along the top.

"Listen carefully," Alice instructed. "If we screw this up we won't get another chance, and the tracks have to be good for it to work. As we get alongside that run of rock on the left of the trail I want to jump onto it. Do it carefully so it doesn't show, just jump sideways onto a rock, and sit there. Rest, and keep lookout. I'm going to turn right at that point. You see that ridge heading off to the right? I'm going to hike out along the base of it, in the snow. It's over a foot deep and it'll make a trail they can't miss. But it's also deep enough so they won't be able to distinguish our cleat marks. To check the size of the footprints. In other words, they won't know you didn't go that way."

"But they will see it's only one set of tracks."

"Right. Stick with me. I'll go out until I get near

that rocky crest. And then I'll angle up to it, like it's easier to walk on the rocks at that point. That ridge goes out quite a ways. And it's clean rock, so they won't be expecting any tracks until the far end of it. But I won't go out to the end. As soon as I get to the rock I'm coming back here, but I'll walk backward. By the time I get back here there will be two sets of tracks going out there. They will both be mine, but they won't know that. Then I'll jump sideways onto your rock and we'll run like hell, parallel to the trail, along these rocks. After we get out a ways, out of sight from here, we can get back on the trail. Do you understand all that?"

Ruth nodded.

"Okay. Then jump up there." Alice watched carefully to make sure it looked right. "Sit tight, rest up, and keep lookout, because when I get back we'll have to go like hell."

Ruth watched her slogging through the snow at the base of the ridge, moving as fast as she could, shrinking as she receded. She went slower after she turned uphill, pausing every few steps to rest, but reaching the top seemed to renew her strength. She didn't stop more than an instant, but backed off the crest almost immediately, walking backward down the hill, looking back to make sure she followed the set of tracks she had just made.

Alice found it harder to walk backward, and awkward to go down the hill that way. Walking backward made a different imprint, with the toe taking the weight, so with each step she tried to lift her toe and set her heel down first, instead of the other way around. The loose snow which was carried by toe and heel as they entered and left the bank was pushed backward instead of forward, but there was nothing she could do about that. And it wasn't obvious. She just hoped they wouldn't notice. It seemed forever before she got back to Ruth, and by then she wished she had found a shorter route for confusing them. She wasn't sure how much strength she had left to actually escape, if this worked. But the tracks were clear and incriminating. Just what she wanted. She leaped sideways and Ruth grabbed and steadied her.

Together they set out again, on the rock ridge now, as quickly as they could manage.

Chuck's back began to tire, but he didn't straighten up. They were jogging along, bent as low as possible, ready to drop in the snow and roll off the trail at the first hint of ambush. It was only the thought of ambush that kept Ryner from running flat out, charging right up their backs. They were both grunting from the awkward exertion, Ryner with his gun out and Chuck with his hand resting tensely on his holster.

Now up another rise. A row of rock paralleled the trail on the left. But the tracks turned right, leaving the trail, running along the base of a ridge for a while and then up to the rocky crest. "They turned off," Chuck said, stopping to catch his breath. Ryner had been right on his flank, checking everything for himself, still leading every minute even though he was hiking behind.

Ryner studied the situation, trying to understand from the tracks and the place what their quarry had been thinking and trying to do. Stretching out long feelers of intuition to make sure that the game had not changed without his knowing it.

He looked pleased at this sign that just running from him was hopeless.

"They may think they can double back behind that ridge and gun us when we get out there. So you follow the tracks. I'll stay here and cover you. Then I'll come out and you'll cover me."

If nothing happens to me first, Chuck thought. But he started out obediently. He felt like a decoy, like the lamb tied in the jungle clearing to draw the tiger. A necessary sacrifice in an important hunt. The deep snow was exhausting and began to soak through his pants almost immediately. He stumbled several times because his eyes wouldn't stay on the trail. He kept glancing up and . . . The roar was harsh, urgent, and unintelligible. Chuck dove into the snow and fumbled for his gun. When he raised his head he saw Ryner high on the rock. Ryner waved him back with a short chop of his hand. The yell came again.

"Get back here!"

As he approached, Ryner scrambled back down the rocks to where they met the trail. "You see this?" he demanded, gloating. His face had reddened like raw meat with his excitement. Chuck looked down past the pointing finger. On the cleanly windswept back of the rock were two small, packed pieces of snow. Ryner picked one up. It was smooth on the sides and flat on top, almost half an inch high and three-quarters of an inch long. He pinched it between his fingers. It didn't crumble easily.

"That fell out of their cleats. They jumped up here and went over the rock. Up higher you can see where they went back to the trail again."

Shit, Chuck thought.

"We got 'em now. They wasted their lead doing this little number. They're close. . . ." And then he added, "Get ready."

"Yeah," Chuck agreed uncomfortably, not knowing for sure what he meant.

"Then get your gun out," Ryner ordered.

The women heard the shout. The force of it was quite clear even though they couldn't make out the words. It was close. On their trail, definitely not far up the ridge where Alice had hoped to mislead them. They were coming again. And now they were very close behind. The women had climbed another rise while running, and then dropped down the other side. Now only that single rise hid them from the men. At any minute they could come over the top and everyone would be exposed, each couple in plain view of the other.

The trail ran up another narrow ridge of rock, and curved to the right, in front of it again. There was no shelter for over a quarter of a mile. Then the path disappeared over the edge. They were reaching the lower end of the basin. Past it the trail followed switchbacks, zigzagging down the steep slope toward the valley below.

When they reached the rocks they decided quickly to go behind them, rather than stay in front and be exposed on the trail. It would not be a secret. Their tracks would tell the story clearly this time. But at least they would be sheltered from any shooting for a while. The ridge looked high and narrow and curved in the same direction as the trail. They would follow behind it and hope to cut back at some point to the trail again, to race down and out of the valley ahead of their pursuers.

There was no chance for any more games. The goal was only to run and keep hidden as long as possible.

They scurried as quickly as they could, not holding anything back, knowing that if this didn't work then they would not need any reserves. Along their right the ridge rose, twenty, thirty feet of granite only an experienced climber could hope to challenge from this side. Alice thought she might have a chance if she were rested and had some equipment. But probably not now. And Ruth, never. They were walled in for the moment.

Then they came to the drop-off. Ahead of them the snow under their feet disappeared and was replaced by sky. They stood at the edge and looked down the steep slope, almost a wall, studded with sharp outcroppings. It looked like a rocky form of barbed wire. There would be no liberating toboggan slide down that. Not without being hacked to death long before reaching the bottom. Better to be captured. Or even shot.

But the ridge continued to curve to the right, and they continued to follow it, waiting for the break, the low point they could climb or the crack they could wriggle through and get back to the trail. They waded on, gasping and struggling through the knee-deep snow as rapidly as they could, ignoring the burn in their lungs and the knots in their thighs, the raw scrape of the packs on their backs. The rocks on their right followed the cliff on their left, twenty feet back, fifteen, curving around so they couldn't see ahead, waiting constantly for their gateway, their escape, but instead being constantly closed in tighter and tighter. The space narrowed down to ten feet. And then abruptly it opened up to fifteen feet again, or twenty, a little clearing bounded by the drop on the left and by the rock on the right. Then the rock curved totally out to the cliff.

They made no comment. They continued driving, the momentum of their desperation carrying them right to the edge where the rock wall touched the lip of the canyon. Alice looked out along the direction they had been fleeing. There was a narrow ledge which extended from where she stood at the edge of the clearing to halfway across the cliff face. Then even that dwindled to nothing and there was only sheer rock. Further to the right and far below they could make out the trail, switchbacking down toward the valley floor, now hopelessly out of reach. Neither of them said a word all this time. It was all before them. There was nothing to say.

There was no way down the several hundred feet of slide and sawtooth which fell beneath their feet. There was no way across. It was impossible to scale the rock wall between them and the trail. And they couldn't go back, unless they wanted to meet the rangers who had been hounding them in bloodlust.

After looking everything over twice, accepting with finality that it was all as it looked, Alice stood at the far edge of the small clearing and studied the partial ledge which lay in front of them.

"You can't possibly make that," Ruth said. "It doesn't even go all the way across. And it's covered with snow, and probably loose rock under that. I don't want you hurt. It's not worth it. I'm sure they'll let us surrender. They'll have to. I don't want you to do something stupid. . . ." Ruth continued to talk, trailing slowly off, repeating herself in a form of exhausted hysteria, babbling to release the panic which fatigue and cold and wet, more than self-control, had reduced to a pathetic dribble of unhappy feeling.

And Alice continued to stare dumbly at the narrow, traitorous ledge which vanished in the middle rather than carrying them to freedom.

They trotted rapidly, bent low like dogs on a scent. As they topped the rise they separated, Chuck going to the right and Ryner to the left, leaving the trail and plowing up through the snow. So when their heads popped over the crest they were not in line with the trail. Just in case someone was waiting for them, hoping to surprise them.

From that point Ryner could see the story written clearly below. They jogged down the slope, tiredness gone, their thrust strong. The tracks were clear. They curved behind the rock wall, leaving the trail unbroken and smooth.

"That doesn't go through," Chuck said, studying the prints.

"No. They're done. There's no way out except back this way," said Ryner. He looked over the situation, wanting to be sure there was no mistake. "You go up," he said to Chuck, pointing at the rock. "This is it. They're not giving up. So we have to take 'em."

Chuck nodded.

"They're waiting for us in there," Ryner snapped. "But if we're smart it won't do them any good." He wiped his nose on the back of his sleeve, gun in hand, catching his breath a bit. "So I want you up there. Cover me this time. I'll go in on their tracks. You go in on the top of the rocks. I want you ahead of me. You look back and see if they're laying for me behind something. And be quiet."

Chuck moved out toward the rock feeling Ryner watching him. He crossed ten feet of snow and came to the stones, small ones, the first low-lying few still snow-covered. Then some bigger ones, like steps to give him a leg up. The next step was much bigger, a stretch as high as he could lift his leg. And then he had to hop up to shift his weight to his high foot. The rock was smooth and felt like it could be slippery, even under his cleats. It could be dangerous, just the climbing, even if no one were waiting below to kill him.

This was not a smooth ridge, but a long, thin jumble of rock. In places he could step from one boulder to another, like rocks in a stream. As he got higher he remembered to look down, checking for ambush points. Ryner! He remembered Ryner and turned to signal that he was on his way, but Ryner was nowhere to be seen. The spot where he had been standing was empty. Tracks led to the base of the rock, and disappeared. In many places Chuck couldn't see over the curve of the stone well enough to check the ground. He had no idea where Ryner stood, or what he was doing.

Looking back he was surprised to see how far he had come. He had been concentrating on every handhold, each foot placement, being quiet and careful, a little bit at a time, and while focusing on the details he had not realized how they added up, how far he had come. This was going faster than he had expected. It could all be over very soon.

He realized then that he might need his gun at

any instant. Automatically, he had holstered it when he began to climb. Now he took it out again, with a strange mixture of feeling. He didn't like it. Yet it was a relief to have it. He felt his hand tighten on the grip, clinging for security. He had a brief urge to fire it wildly in the air, to scare them away, so they could go home and forget about all this.

He didn't want to kill them. But also he didn't want them to kill him. He was afraid it was heading toward a choice between either one or the other. He was trapped just like they were. And he might have to shoot just to defend himself. If you could call it self-defense when you hunted someone and cornered them. And what, he wondered, if he just saw someone with a gun? Someone with their back to him, or sideways even, but not seeing him yet. For the first time he wondered what he would do. He knew the right answer, the answer he would have given in town. He should call loudly and firmly, "Drop that gun, I'm a U.S. ranger and I've got you covered. Throw down your gun and put your hands up."

Up on that rock, with the wind cold and the sky unloving, it sounded silly. They could turn and shoot him as easily as he could shoot them. He knew that from any distance, with any movement and excitement, and shooting from above, from a bad angle, he was as likely to miss as to hit what he shot at. They would have as good a chance at hitting him. Except it wasn't a "hit." There was no word that really told what happened when a bullet came into your body. And what if he had no cover, sitting up on some smooth rock? It would be safer to shoot, to kill whomever he saw, as soon as he could. And where the hell was Ryner?

There was a gap between his rock and the next. He could climb down four or five feet and then try to scramble up the six or seven feet to the next top, an uncomfortable-looking, difficult climb. Or he could jump. He took his finger off the trigger and jumped. He landed with an unpleasant thud, full length against the rock, fingers and toes digging in for a hold. It didn't work. Wind knocked out of him, sore chest and skinned knuckles, he slid down into the cleft. He rested a minute, but the stillness only emphasized his pains and fears, so he started the climb. He tried several times, different ways, but it was too slippery to go forward so he finally gave up and climbed back on the rock he had stood on before. Again he jumped, putting extra effort into it, smashed himself against the rock again, banged his knuckles again, concentrating on making the jump so intently that he didn't have attention left to protect himself from such little troubles.

He made it this time, locking himself to the side so he didn't fall back, and he could scramble up to the top after a minute. His gun was freezing in his hand. He could see his knuckles were scraped, bright against his pale fingers, and little fringes of torn skin were standing out around the edges. His fingers were stiff from the cold and the banging, and it was clumsy to hold the gun. But he didn't holster it again. Because I need it. Because I don't have a big sign on my chest saying: Please Don't Shoot Me Because I Am One Hell Of A Nice Guy. He saw Ryner now, twenty yards behind and al-

most thirty feet below, sliding his bulk along
against the wall for as much cover as he could get.

The rock against his back felt cold and clammy, but his body was hot and coated with sweat.
He padded silently through the deep snow. They
know I'm coming. But they won't know when,
Ryner figured. Something tightened another notch
in his guts. The tension was an unpleasant pleasure. The release would be when he could finally
rush out shooting. But he didn't know when that
would be. It could be blindingly, confusingly, sur-
prisingly sudden, and he had to be constantly
ready. What a relief it would be to release himself,
not to hold back anymore, to let it all come out
naturally.

He hadn't felt this way since that other time.
The elk hunt. Or "the last hunt" as he called it bit-
terly to himself. Because he hadn't been hunting
since that time, hadn't felt he could ask anyone,
hadn't known anyone who wasn't touched by the
cloud, and he didn't like to hunt alone.

Three of them had hunted, now and then, for
years. They had played cards and gotten drunk and
even gone to whores a couple of times. But since
that last hunt they had avoided each other, without discussion. Ryner had said they shouldn't tell
anyone. People wouldn't understand. Feeling
strange, they all agreed. But someone had talked
anyway.

*It had been a hunt, like lots of hunts, like hunts
often were. They had brought a lot of food and
plenty to drink. Bourbon was what they all favored.
Steaks and bourbon, the proper nourishment for
hunting men. They made camp along the river.
They got drunk. The steaks burned and he didn't*

like that, annoyed at one of the others for not watching them, but he held it in. It was a hunt and he didn't want to start arguing. They played some cards. They sloshed each other with whiskey. They broke empty bottles against trees. They fired into the darkness to scare away evil spirits. To keep bears far away from camp. Drunk as they were, they didn't want anybody or anything coming around to take advantage of them. It may have been good that they did, for one of the men passed out on the ground and didn't drag himself into the tent, half-frozen and sick to his stomach, until it was almost dawn. And lucky he had done himself no permanent damage.

They slept late, later than they should have, and woke with big heads and bad bodies. Their breath seemed to catch like slime on the stubble of their unshaven faces. Ryner hated to go without shaving, but no one shaved when hunting and he didn't feel able to go against the custom. Coffee helped their heads a little, but made their stomachs gurgle unpleasantly. They made several trips into the bushes, the coffee draining through them in a hot bitter flush of insubstantial lumps in an acid broth, spattering on the ground, burning the ass, unpleasant even as it left. The wreckage of the camp was depressing also, so as soon as they could, they set out.

They had automatic weapons. His was the Savage 30-06, he remembered. His elk rifle. They started up a small tributary, heading deeper into back country. But they were blocked, and that further annoyed them. The stream poured from a cliff. They couldn't scale it and had to make a long detour. As they went on, the underbrush grew denser. It was harder to walk. Bushes scratched them, face and hands, caught at the rifles, and tripped them. One man tore a gash in his down jacket and feathers poured out, no one having any tape to stop the flow. Deeper, and denser. And soon they realized they would have trouble getting close to any living thing, wading through the brush as they were. And even if they did flush something worth shooting, it would be almost impossible to get a shot off. One frustration on top of another, and no sign that anything was going to get any better.

That was when they found the elk. They almost fell on top of them. Circling around, almost forgetting that they were looking for the stream, they suddenly and unexpectedly reached it. The water flowed through a small canyon thirty feet below them. It was frozen over now, and snow-covered, or the elk wouldn't have been there. The walls were steep, the other side only fifty feet away. Downstream was a waterfall. The entrance was along the frozen stream from above. It was a small group, seven or eight. They were browsing on the bark and bushes along the edge, on the branches which hung down over the ice. They were relaxed and felt safe. They had not smelled or heard the men.

The hunters above them had not had a shot all morning. Everything had defeated them, no matter what they tried. Now, as if to make up for that, suddenly there was enough shooting, enough to gorge themselves on, enough to satisfy them and make up for the pain in the head and the bowels, the bitter taste in the mouth and the hard climb and the stupid underbrush.

He fired. He thought he fired. Even now he didn't have any distinct memory of shooting first, but somehow he felt he must have. By implication. Because of everything that had happened since then. No. Even though there was no proof in his mind, no reasonable calculations to spell it out, he was sure in his heart that he fired first. Because he could still feel the long terrible rush of the release.

It was one continuous roar, three semiautomatics firing rapidly, as quickly and as much as anyone could want, aim and shoot, like a gallery with moving targets, no holding back from the satisfaction they wanted, hot shells popping up, the tangy, burnt smell, animals falling, the shrieking of the wounded, the bellowing of the terrified, an old buck down early, turning to face the danger when he saw they were trapped, a young doe trying hopelessly to climb the wall, falling back when she was hit, blood coming from nowhere, from everywhere, to spot the snow.

One wounded animal trying to crawl away, evidently hit in the spine, back legs stiff and useless, trying to hunch over its front feet, not realizing how useless it all was. He dropped his last slug into it, hitting the neck, not a clean-killing shot but something that would take a little time. Seeing it lying there, just twitching now, feebly, with little movements of its forehooves, like a dog's dream of running. And then the realization that he had been the last to fire as well as the first, the others already stopped, and registering the slaughter below them, watching him empty his magazine. And then just the stunning silence.

It was still real. He could still see it and feel it,

as if it were here as much as there. And it was. Because it was in him and he was here and he could still feel it. Feel it as he did around the last rock almost sick with excitement. Still seeing the last animal trying vainly to get to its feet, not realizing that it was all over, that its back legs would never work again and it was time to die. He raised his gun and then Chuck's screaming filled the air. "Don't shoot! Don't shoot, Ryner, please don't shoot!" he pleaded as Ryner almost emptied his .38 into the thin blond woman huddled in the snow before Chuck's voice registered.

Chuck had gotten there first. High on his rock, able to look down into the clearing, he had an overview which shocked him. One woman slumped back against a rock. It looked at first like sitting, but it was too formless a posture to be called that. She was a thin woman with pale skin, skin that now was turning a soft, sickly blue, like the snow shadows around her. She twitched from time to time and seemed to be mumbling incoherently to herself. Her rifle lay in the snow near her, but she seemed incapable of reaching for it, or even of understanding that it was there. As he watched she sagged over sideways, the rock no longer supporting her, her face falling half into the snow.

The other one was already dead. If she was lucky. She had tried to cross the ledge which projected partway across the cliff at the end of the clearing. It was a hopeless gesture anyway, since the ledge didn't reach. Chuck felt a surge of shame that they had driven them in this way. He could see a bright parka, half-buried in the snow below. After she had fallen, he supposed that the other woman waited for them, her rifle out, ready to de-

fend herself for the last time. But it looked as if
exhaustion and cold, hypothermia, had taken over
before they arrived. And she had dropped her gun.
Or even thrown it away. Waiting there hopeless
and alone, slowly freezing to death, until she didn't
care or didn't know, and so collapsed. For the first
time, now that she was real, he wondered who she
was, what she was like. He was sorry. He was truly
sorry it had come to this.

And then Ryner had come into the clearing,
gun out and ready to shoot. And he had screamed,
afraid that what was already horrible would now
turn bizarre. But Ryner had heard him, at the last
minute, and had not fired.

Ryner walked quickly over to her, picked up the
rifle, and popped the clip. He dropped that in his
pocket and then he threw the rest away where it
would be no threat. He walked to the cliff edge
and looked down. What a way to go. It was halfway between a fall and a slide, down over jagged
rock for at least a hundred and fifty feet. Like getting your foot caught in a stirrup and being
dragged over rocky ground by a frightened horse,
ripped up and pounded to death. He had always
been afraid something like that might happen to
him. He was always careful when he rode. So it
fascinated him to see someone else who hadn't
been. He wondered how long she had been con-
scious, how much she had known what was happening, what she thought. She was mostly buried
under a small slide of rock and snow she had
dragged with her. Her torn jacket was clearly
visible though. And the money.

Loose bills were scattered below. Her pack
could not be seen. It was buried somewhere near-

by. The money was starting to blow away and he watched the gray-green papers flutter down toward the valley. Caught in an updraft one of the bills blew near his feet, stuck to the snow briefly, flapping, and then blew away again. It was only a single. How stupid to steal dollar bills. Even thousands of them. And die for them. Perhaps he shouldn't have run them so hard. Broken them. They weren't worth all that effort. If he had realized that, he could have just grabbed them. And dragged them back whole.

Chuck scrambled slowly down the rock, extra careful now that there was no reason to take chances anymore. He used both hands, his gun holstered again, and felt much more comfortable, more natural that way. Ryner kept an eye on the woman, but she only moaned from time to time, and moved little.

"Well, that's that," he said when Chuck finally made it.

"Jesus."

Only now that they were both there and ready did Ryner chance frisking the woman. He walked over carefully, still wary of surprise, and shoved her quickly onto her back. She groaned but did not resist. He patted her down but the only lump he found was in her pants pocket. It felt too small to be dangerous, but he worked it out anyway, struggling with her limpness and weight. It was a Swiss army knife, new-looking, probably bought just for this trip. It was a good model, with lots of clever attachments, useful in the woods. He confiscated it, slipping it into his pocket without a word. She wouldn't need it.

Chuck propped her up, trying to get her sitting

even though she was just a mess of twitches and flops like some inflatable toy collapsing. He felt her cold, blue fingers and tried to find a pulse, something he had never been successful at.

Ryner watched him without much interest and then reached over and pushed her parka hood off her head. He grabbed her firmly by the hair and gave a cruel yank. Ruth's head only jerked on the limp line that was her neck, able to resist nothing anymore. "Well, at least this one's a woman. No wig," he sneered. He enjoyed the feel of his fingers buried in those soft blond curls and would have liked to pull again. Because of Chuck he didn't. There were over a hundred men in this county, all looking as hard as they could for these people. And he was the first to know for sure if this one was a man or a woman.

"She's really bad," Chuck said. "We're not going to get her out alive."

Ryner glanced briefly at him, not really interested. He was annoyed at the implicit demand that they do something to help her. He didn't owe her anything. She signed up for trouble when she started this. She shouldn't be surprised she got it. It wasn't his lookout.

He spotted her pack nearby. He went over while Chuck fumbled with the woman, trying to decide what to do. He untied the laces and lifted the top flap. It was full of money. He whistled through his teeth. It would be nice to have it. The thought occurred to him that he had the robbery gun. If he were to shoot Chuck with that, and then shoot the woman with his own gun . . . But that was too tricky. He was too tired to be that ambitious.

"We've got to do something," Chuck urged.

"Feels like she's headed into core-cooling and she won't have long after that."

"Sure. You work with her and I'll go down and check the other one." He could backtrack around the rocks, take the trail to the bottom of the cliff, and climb back up to reach her from there. Maybe he could tuck a little money behind a rock while he was at it. No one could ever prove anything about that. And he could come back for it later.

"You've got to help me. I can't do this myself," Chuck insisted.

It all seemed so simple for him, Ryner thought. It never occurred to him that they didn't have to do a thing if they didn't want to. When he got to the bottom, if the other woman was still alive he wouldn't say a thing to Chuck. She'd die soon enough, naturally. Let her cool. He'd help Chuck first.

"What do you want to do?" Ryner asked.

Chuck untied her sleeping bag from her pack and spread it on the snow next to her. They sat her on it, getting her off the ground for the first time, and started to strip her. It was awkward work, and they were slow and clumsy with her limp body. She was no help and a confused weight. First they untied her hiking boots, pulling the laces almost totally free before they could get them off her feet. And her socks. It probably would have been better to leave them for last, to preserve as much heat as they could, but they weren't that well organized, Chuck realized. They would have to do the best they could. Her parka came off easily, the zipper just a single stroke, and the shell peeling with a pull on one cuff and then the other. The buttons on her wool shirt took longer, and her head kept flopping over so her chin was in the way. They stripped her longies. She seemed to have delicate skin, he thought sympathetically. She had no bra. She was a skinny thing, long-bodied, with her ribs showing a bit. Her nipples darkened and crinkled as soon as the cold air hit them. She groaned again.

"This one needed the falsies just to look like a woman," Ryner snorted.

They had to hoist her up now. Ryner held her while Chuck worked. Ryner found that unpleasant, gripping her tensely under her arms. Chuck undid her belt and pulled her pants and long johns down in one motion. He left her panties on. There was no need. She looked so vulnerable swaying there in Ryner's unsympathetic clutch, naked in the mountain clearing, long, sticklike legs, beanpole body caving in, naturally pale, and almost ghostly in that light, in that place. Pitiful clump of pubic hair showing through her panties, a small fuzzy flag to decorate a warmth which was now fading, going out. Elbows sharp. Shoulder blades like underdeveloped wings. Spine . . .

They stuffed her, with difficulty, into her sleeping bag.

"You?" Chuck asked.

"No. It was your idea. You do it."

Chuck, stripping quickly on the mountaintop, was a strong contrast. Healthy, pink, and solid. He uncovered down to his jockey shorts and slid in with her.

"Okay, I'm going down to get the money. Be back as soon as I can."

Chuck screamed first.

"Help! Help! Help!" he hollered, hysterical, his

voice climbing in pitch as he went on, abandoning all control in his panic.

"Now! Alice! Do it now! Get him now!" Ruth screamed, the cords standing out on her throat.

Ryner snapped back, drawing his gun. No way he could get a clear shot with them thrashing around in the bag on the snow. And even if he plugged her in the back, the .38 slug would go right through and into Chuck.

"Help! She's got me!" Chuck screamed wildly, terrified that this corpse returned from the brink and clutched him for God knew what reason. She caught him helpless in a naked hug. Delirious. Terrifying.

Ryner aimed, straining for his opening.

Behind him a snow-covered hillock at the edge of the clearing rose suddenly upward. First a canopy of sleeping bag appeared, then Alice's face, one dark eye cracked freakishly, as she struggled to her knees with the snow and the bag still over her, like some great hooded cobra rising to strike. And then the gun, the AR-7, ugly and blunt and pointed straight at Ryner's huge back.

"Don't move!" she shrieked, adding her rapid yells to the confusion already curdling the peace in the clearing. "Don't move!" knowing now by Ryner's stiffness that he heard her, and knew she was right behind him. "I mean it, don't move. Put that down," she talk-screamed. "You drop that now! Because I'm telling you I'm scared. I've never been so scared! And I'm tired! I'm sick and tired of you chasing us! So if you make one move I'm going to shoot you, shoot you right away, and think about it later. Now drop that! DROP THAT!"

There was a frozen minute. Ruth and Chuck

stopped and watched, still tightly entwined but no longer struggling. The silence ended gently, by the muted sound of Ryner's gun falling in the snow.

"Okay. Now take off *your* pants," Alice commanded. "And your jacket. I'm getting cold and my jacket is down that cliff, stuffed full of snow."

"Get my knife back. That creep stole my knife," Ruth said scornfully.

"You heard me," Alice hardened her voice just a bit. "Get undressed. Move!"

Monday 5:50 P.M.

Teton campground was quiet. A soft snow was falling in the dusk. No one was outside. But rows of stubborn vehicles held their places. Everyone knew there was some kind of struggle on the mountain. A lot of people who should have been on their way were hanging around, waiting to see how it all turned out.

Norman made some more coffee on the stove in the van. He hadn't thought about eating all day. He made several trips to the wooden outhouse in the center of the campground, each time hurrying and cursing his bladder, as if it would matter if he were there or not, as if there were anything left for him to do.

Returning from one of these trips he heard a hushed call. "There's someone coming!" His heart racing, he rushed back to see.

People poured out of vehicles all around him, but the uncertainty of the situation kept them silent. Seeing the crowd rush toward the trail head, the sheriff turned and blocked them with a curt gesture of his open hand. They stopped short and huddled together to wait and see.

The sheriff and his deputy drew their guns and held them back, low against their hips. They crouched and started up, keeping off the trail and against the dense undergrowth along the side.

After a minute Norman saw them holster the guns, stand up, and step out onto the trail. Two figures approached from the darkened valley and the four of them stood there talking intently.

"I hope they're all right," Carol Baker said. Norman hadn't noticed her near him in the crowd. Her husband stood next to her with their little daughter seated high on his shoulders.

As the four started back toward the camp someone cried out, "It's them! It's the rangers!"

Hours of tension were suddenly released. The little girl began to wave her hands. Feeling the emotion of the crowd flowing through her, and with a child's spontaneity she began to cheer. Spreading like sparks in a wheat field the crowd went up with her.

All but Norman, who craned miserably to see what was happening. The rangers looked tired, exhausted, but relieved. The sheriff continued to question them earnestly as they came into the campground.

As they drew closer Norman saw the tall ranger pull off the distinctive hat and give a high, pale forehead a wipe with the back of a jacket sleeve. He had been clapping feebly, trying to blend in, the crowd's cry unsettling in his ears. When her blond curls sprang out he recognized Ruth immediately. And then the cracked lens in Alice's glasses. He felt a shiver go through him. Now he began to cheer in earnest.

"My God, they're women!" Carol gasped.

"You bet they are!" Norman shouted back with satisfaction.

The sheriff raised his hands, trying vainly to quiet the crowd. "Okay, folks, it's all over. False alarm. Nothing's going to be happening here to-night. We have to wait for the other two rangers to come through, but you can all go home now. I want you to leave in an orderly fashion. Drive carefully. And can anyone give these ladies a lift back to the park?"

Several hands shot up but the women solved the problem by simply walking over to Norman. They fought to keep from meeting each other's eyes. Norman strained to look casual, leading them back to the van. He helped them strip their packs off and drop them in the back.

"Hmmmm, heavy!" was all he said, without look-ing up.

They climbed again into the familiar old van. Motors were starting and headlights flashing all around them. Everyone was hurrying to get away now, and Norman eased out into the line of traffic as soon as there was an opening. He stared straight ahead. They took the first bend on the gravel road and some trees cut them off from the campground. The excitement of relief kept building, Norman's knuckles turning white as he gripped the steering wheel. When it started it started low and deep in his chest and became bigger and bigger until when it reached his throat it was a tremendous yell that filled the van, a deluge of strapped-up fear and worry that had compounded itself all day long, and as it poured out it ignited them all.

"WE DID IT, WE DID IT, WE REALLY DID IT!" screamed Alice.

"OH, MY GOD, OH, MY GOD!" Ruth yelled.

"NORMAN, YOU WAITED, ALL THAT TIME YOU WAITED," yelled Alice.

"NORMAN, NORMAN, NORMAN," yelled Ruth.

They were screaming and hugging and kissing Norman, who was yelling and trying to keep the van on the road.

"My God, my God, my God," Norman moaned in the ecstasy of release.

Ruth hung her tongue and rolled her eyes like an exhausted dog. Then they all hugged again and hollered some more, just to let it out and because it felt so good.

"I'm so glad to see you two," said Norman, his eyes wet with joy.

"Oh, you waited for us, all that time you waited for us," said Alice and hugged him again.

"Are you two all right?"

"I think so, yes! And we have the money. All but a few hundred singles we threw over a cliff. Oh, we have a lot to tell you!" said Ruth.

"Where to now?" Norman asked. "I want to get the hell out of here."

"Idaho Falls," said Ruth. "We have one little bit of unfinished business to take care of as soon as it's safe. And we'd better change out of these uniforms right away."

Monday 7:29 P.M.

Diane dropped Mike at his dorm and watched him trudge sullenly into the building. Well, maybe tomorrow. Maybe they could make up over breakfast before he flew back. Then she turned for home. She would soothe herself with a tall scotch while she sat in a hot tub.

But when she got there a note was tacked to her door. "Diane, check with Bill at Moose," it read. She sighed and climbed back in the car.

She parked in the lot behind headquarters. A pale green station wagon was there, abandoned and partially pulled apart. Sheets were spread on the asphalt all around it and lying on them were the parts which had been torn from the car: the seats, ashtrays, floor mats, the red light from the roof, the contents of the glove compartment, piles of sweepings and vacuumings from the corners and crevices. All the doors had been left open and the small inside light stayed on. In the darkness that gave it an eerie touch, like one of those ghost ships which are sometimes found drifting, inexplicably abandoned in the open sea with food still untouched on the table.

The tempo was practically back to normal but the room was still littered with papers and coffee

251

cups. Bill had his feet up, reading a newspaper at his desk. He noticed her as soon as she came in. "Hi. What are you doing here?"

"There was a note on my cabin."

"Oh, yeah," he remembered. "I forgot all about it. That was just to satisfy that agent. The one from the FBI. He kept pushing me to get ahold of you. To talk about some theory you had. Remember? Well, he went over to Idaho to take custody and I just forgot to have it taken down. You heard we got 'em, didn't you?"

"Were they all right?"

He looked puzzled by the question. "I'm waiting to hear myself. The sheriff is going to give me a call as soon as he gets it wrapped up." He was quite pleased with himself.

"I located the car. And we found"—he picked up a report from the desk and scanned it—"Uh ... dog hairs, wigs, rib-stop tape, et cetera, et cetera, et cetera ... falsies," he added and glanced up significantly. He opened a drawer, took out a manila envelope, and shook several small items onto his blotter. "Stove key. *Backpack* stove key," he emphasized, "and this." With his finger he tapped a book of matches from the White Swallow bar.

"Incongruous as it might sound," he announced, "the lodge was robbed by three men, who then hiked out of here."

"What!"

He looked at her face, waiting for the realization to strike, but she evidently needed help. "Don't you see? It explains everything. The robbery. The getaway. Why we were confused and couldn't anticipate anything they did. They weren't three women. They were three men. Fags! Oh, excuse me," he said patronizingly, "I mean gay people. You were guessing something like that," he remembered vaguely. "You know, you were probably a lot closer than you realized."

She exploded. "WHAT DO YOU MEAN, I GUESSED!" she shouted in his face, leaning across the desk and suddenly not caring to control herself anymore. "God damn it! I know what happened. I figured it out and I told you." She jabbed dangerously at him with her finger. "But *you* wouldn't listen! *You* . . ."

There was a ring and every head in the office swung from the argument to the phone.

Bill started to reach for it, but a meek voice from across the room said, "Uh, no, it's for you, Diane. On three."

She pulled the receiver brusquely from his desk and turned her back to him. No one was looking at anyone else and Bill felt his cheeks tingling.

When she hung up and turned back she looked solid again. Even detached. "That was a woman," she said evenly. "Two rangers are tied in sleeping bags behind a ridge over Devil's Staircase. And if we don't want them to freeze we'd better get them out tonight. They said, if you can't find them, just follow the tracks. . . . And bring some clothes," she added. "They've lost their jackets, shoes, and pants."

"Get me the sheriff's office," Bill called after a long minute, but he had to say it twice before he could make himself heard.

He watched Diane cross the room. As she got to the door he called out, stopping her before she left, "Diane, how did they know to ask for you by name?" He watched her face suspiciously across the distance and listened for the tone as much as the answer itself.

"I haven't the faintest idea," she said flatly, and stepped out into the fresh night air. The moon was heavy and radiant. In its light she suddenly thought everything had become unusually clear.

Great detective novels "in the American private-eye tradition of Chandler, Hammet and MacDonald."
—NEW YORK TIMES BOOK REVIEW

MICHAEL COLLINS MYSTERIES